"*I* think you are a fool, sir," Susan said clearly. "And a bounder, as well."

"What's this?" Sir Rupert demanded. "You go too far, Miss Eaton. I will not be made a cake of!"

"Then let me go!" Susan demanded. "If you do not, you shall hear a few more home truths, I assure you. Enough, I fancy, to convince you that I am no tease."

"Come now, you know you fancy me," Sir Rupert said in a rough voice. "No need to draw away from me like that. Intentions honorable, and all that sort of thing. Mean to offer for you, if you'll let me get a word in edgewise, and that's a fact. Set the village on its ear, we will, my little lovely."

And, as Susan stared at him, appalled, he reached out for her. In an instant she was struggling in his bearlike embrace. She could not cry out or make a sound. But her eyes were clear. And then, in a moment of horror, she found herself looking straight into Lord Woodstone's face. . . .

Franklin's Folly

Georgina Grey

FAWCETT COVENTRY • NEW YORK

FRANKLIN'S FOLLY

Published by Fawcett Coventry Books, a unit of CBS Publications, the Consumer Publishing Division of CBS Inc.

ISBN: 0-449-50026-8

Printed in the United States of America

First Fawcett Coventry Printing: February 1980

10 9 8 7 6 5 4 3 2 1

For Kinley and Christopher

CHAPTER

One

"*The fact remains that* either you or papa must do something about Franklin at once, Mama!"

Mrs. Eaton turned to her daughter with a look of dismay which expressed as well as words her reluctance to attempt to do anything about her only son, about whom she understood very little except that he showed a marked distaste for helping his father administer his small estate, showing instead an extraordinary preference for puttering about with the astrological equipment on which he spent every shilling he could lay his hands on.

"I think that if you wish to have a serious talk about your brother, my dear, you must go to your father," Mrs. Eaton said with a flutter of her small, plump hands. "You know as well as I that I have never been able to do anything about Franklin."

"Papa would only shrug his shoulders and laugh," Susan protested.

"Then perhaps that is what you should do, my dear," her mother suggested, her eyes wandering around the little sitting room in their usual vagrant manner. "I am certain that Franklin will be terribly annoyed if he guesses that you want to interfere. After all, it *is* an affair of the heart."

Susan shook her head so vehemently that the blue ribbon which moored her thick, black curls threatened to become dislodged.

"It is an affair of *his* heart, Mama," she declared, "which is precisely what troubles me. I cannot bear to see him hurt and humiliated."

Since there was no one in the village of Thrumhill who held his head higher than Squire Eaton, it was not surprising that his only daughter should hold the honor of the family in such high regard. This, at least, was what Mrs. Eaton always told herself when Susan threatened to become troublesome. As for herself, she was willing to live and let live, if for no other reason than that this was a philosophy which allowed her to be very little troubled about the way other people lived their lives. It had been her experience, as she was fond of telling anyone who would listen, that people must make their own mistakes with as little interference as possible.

"If only Lord Woodstone had not chosen to play at being a gentleman farmer," Susan an-

8

nounced, struggling with the recalcitrant ribbon. She was a handsome girl whose face held too much character to be called beautiful, particularly when, as now, her green eyes glittered with anger. "We were all very well here until he and his family came to Muir Hall and set everything sideways."

"I had not noticed that anything is much changed, my dear," her mother said soothingly. "And as for 'sideways,' I think you go too far."

Susan began to pace the room so rapidly that the sprigged muslin of her full skirt billowed about her.

"Oh, Mama, why do you always prefer to close your eye to anything that might mean the least unpleasantness?" she demanded. "Everyone in the village is in a perfect fit of impatience waiting for Lady Woodstone to take some notice of them, and yet I know for a fact that she sees fit never to be at home when someone calls."

Mrs. Eaton's plump face puckered like a pink pincushion.

"Well, of course, my dear, a distinguished person like Lady Woodstone must exercise some discrimination when she forms her associations. After all, she has been accustomed to the very cream of London Society. And, as for receiving no one, that is an exaggeration, surely, unless you consider that our family counts for very little."

"As for Lady Woodstone's being distinguished," Susan said warmly, "I found her to be a disagreeable old party who would condescend to the King of England if she were given the opportunity. And, as for inviting us to Muir Hall, you know she only did so because of Papa's north meadow which her son wishes to rent."

As always when she was forced to turn her attention to reality, Mrs. Easton placed herself very carefully in her favorite wingchair near the fire and, picking up her embroidery hoop, began to stab at the pattern indiscriminately.

"Tell me, my dear," she said absently, "do you think I should do this bit in pink or red, for I confess I have never really noticed the color of a robin's eyes."

But Susan was not to be put off so easily.

"And, as for Maria Woodstone," she said, "which is more to the point, I do not believe I have ever met such a flitter-flutter person in my life. I declare, I believe she cannot help herself from flirting quite outrageously with every gentleman she meets. Even Papa . . ."

"Oh, my, I think you are quite mistaken there, my dear," Mrs. Eaton said in an agitated manner, giving a little shriek as she drove the needle into her thumb, "for you know as well as I that it would be quite impossible for anyone to flirt with your father. Even as quite a young girl I realized that he never gave a notice to that sort of nonsense. Although," she added inconsequentially, "I am sure Miss Woodstone is pretty enough."

"If she had not been pretty, Franklin would not have lost his head," Susan said, settling herself restlessly on the footstool at her mother's feet. "Had she not been pretty *and* a flirt to boot, for I declare, after her attempt to fascinate Papa, you would have thought no one but Franklin was in the room."

"La, she was just amusing herself as young ladies will," Mrs. Eaton said comfortably. "Why, if this had been London, I am sure no one would have taken any notice."

"But that is just the point, Mama!" Susan cried, springing to her feet. "This is *not* London and I assure you that Lady Woodstone *did* take notice. And her son, as well. And they were *not* amused. Surely you must have noticed the pains they went to to ridicule Franklin when he would insist on going on about his new telescope."

Mrs. Eaton heaved a great sigh and threw a wistful look at the sitting room door, no doubt in the hope that the squire would arrive home early for his tea and put an end to this disturbing discussion.

"You know I would not trouble you with this, Mama, unless I thought it was of the utmost importance," Susan said gently, bending to kiss one plump, pink cheek. "Come, did you not think that Lord Woodstone was as arrogant as his mother?"

"Why, as for that," Mrs. Eaton said helplessly, abandoning embroidery hoop and needle, "I thought he was a handsome fellow and . . ."

"All the village thinks that," Susan said with heavy irony, "particularly every mother with an eligible daughter, although why they should ever dream that he would interest himself in one of us I cannot imagine."

"It does no harm for mamas to dream, my dear," Mrs. Eaton told her. "Besides, there is little enough excitement in Thrumhill."

"But does it not humiliate you to think that at this very moment Mrs. Jackson is planning an entertainment at the village hall in the hope that Lord Woodstone will condescend to put in an appearance? Why, she is having both Ruth and Priscilla fitted for new gowns!"

"Perhaps the Jackson girls *are* a bit long in the tooth to draw the gentleman's attention," Mrs. Eaton admitted. "But they will have the pleasure of hoping for a dance, will they not, and surely that is worth a good deal."

"It is worth a good deal more that they will be sorely disappointed," Susan said grimly. "Besides, Lord Woodstone is a good deal too proud to attend a village dance."

"I cannot think what has turned you so against him, my dear," her mother said with another sigh, "for I found him pleasant enough. He asked your father all manner of questions about farming and I could not blame him for being puzzled when Franklin insisted on going on so about Galileo."

"Very well," Susan said in a low, determined voice. "Perhaps I am mistaken about the manner the gentleman took to my brother. But I think I am right about his mother."

12

"Perhaps she was not quite as genial as one might have wished," Mrs. Eaton admitted. "But then, I believe from what she said that she was not at all pleased to have had to leave London at the height of the Season."

"From the way Lord Woodstone kept his eye on his sister, I think I can guess the reason for it," Susan said thoughtfully. "If she conducted herself in London salons the way she did in the drawing room at Muir Hall, I can only guess at the reputation she might have been in the process of making for herself. No doubt he insisted on her coming here because he saw some misalliance on the horizon."

"I think I hear your father coming," Mrs. Eaton said hopefully.

"It was only Betty in the pantry," Susan assured her. "But come. You must help me. How can Franklin be prevented from making a fool of himself?"

"La, my dear, you have not told me yet how he intends to do that," her mother said, settling her lace cap more securely on her white hair.

"Dear Mama," Susan said, covering her impatience with a smile. "I thought I had made that quite clear when we began this discussion."

"Why, I do not think you could have done so," Mrs. Eaton said, making a bewildered appeal with her violet eyes. "But then you know what a flutterbrain I am."

"That is only what you pretend to be when it suits you," Susan told her fondly.

"That is only because I think it is a mistake to see too much too clearly," her mother confessed, pouting prettily. "But of course I may be wrong."

"You would wrap me around your little finger just as you do Papa," her daughter told her, "and well you know it. But you must be serious about this, Mama, for you do not want to see Franklin hurt any more than I do."

"You think he means to offer for Miss Woodstone, then?" Mrs. Eaton said in a low voice, seeing that guile would take her no further. "But surely you must be wrong, since he has only seen the young lady once."

"What would you say if I told you that his telescope had remained with its wrap on it since that day?" Susan demanded.

"Why, I should think it very odd," her mother confessed.

"And if I should tell you that every evening just at dusk he moons about the gateway to Muir Hall?"

"Perhaps he is looking at stars, my dear."

"If so he could not have chosen a more unlikely place," Susan said dryly, "since the willows grow so thick there that you cannot see the sky."

"A small infatuation," her mother suggested hopefully. "No doubt it will do him good, for I have often thought your brother too serious by far with all his talk of galaxies and such like."

"His appetite has left him, Mama."

14

"It is true that he gave very little attention to Betty's apple tart at dinner."

"And his lamp is kept lit until all hours."

"Now that you mention it, my dear, I thought he looked a bit dark under the eyes this morning. But, still, that does not mean . . ."

"Less than an hour ago I happened to hear him reciting his proposal when I passed his room," Susan said, offering her concluding argument.

Her mother looked around the room help-lessly, as though some ghostly presence might have arrived to make rebuttal.

"How amused Miss Woodstone will be if he suddenly arrives at Muir Hall to make an offer," Susan said grimly. "It is not as though Franklin were some London fop. You know as well as I that his head has never been turned before."

"I had always hoped that he would notice the high regard in which Jane Dawson holds him," Mrs. Eaton said wistfully.

"The fact is that he thinks of Jane much as though she were a second sister," Susan replied briskly. "And now, Mama, we must face facts and think of some way to keep Franklin at arm's length from his own folly."

CHAPTER
Two

*M*uir Hall was an imposing Palladian structure set in a perfect cup of a valley not quite a mile from the village of Thrumhill. Built half a century before by Lord Muir, a crusty old gentleman who valued his privacy, it was surrounded first by a broad expanse of lawn, and then by a circle of willows which, in their turn, were encompassed by a high stone wall which presented a forbidding face to the country road which rambled past it.

Old Lord Muir was now long dead and his son, a fashionable gentleman, not finding himself much attuned to a bucolic existence, was eager enough to rent the place to anyone prepared to pay the formidable fee which residence in such an imposing home demanded.

However, it was not the house itself which

made an appeal to young Lord Woodstone, but rather the adjacent farmland which was part of the bargain. Perhaps it was because his own family estate in Yorkshire offered little in the way of fertility, consisting as it did of a vast expanse of barren, windblown moorland, that the gentleman in question had early on conceived a notion that he would like, of all things, to be a gentleman farmer. With this in mind, he had been careful to obtain from Lord Muir the assurance that, were his project to be as successful as he hoped, an arrangement to purchase could be made, a possibility which Lady Woodstone found as disturbing as her son found it exhilarating.

"You must remember, James," she said as they wandered through the overgrown rose garden in the late afternoon, "that your sister and I prefer polite Society. In a month or more it would be quite proper for us to spend a few weeks with you in the country, since no one of any consequence remains in London through July. But the fact is you have put us in a kind of exile which I, for one, find most annoying."

It was not the first time Lord Woodstone had heard such protestations and he could not be blamed for wearing a distracted expression. A tall young man, wearing the topboots and buckskin breeches in which he now preferred to spend his days, his dark eyes were fixed on the overgrown flower beds as he calculated the number of gardeners who should be employed to put things right.

"I do not believe you are attending to me, James!" his mother exclaimed, unsnapping her fan and passing it back and forth in front of her sharp nose, much like a swordsman flourishing his rapier. Indeed the comparison did not end there for, despite a thick overlay of silk and lace, Lady Woodstone had the narrow figure of a man and it was said by her enemies, of whom she had a great sufficiency, that there was a good deal about her face to remind them of a bust of Julius Caesar in his later years.

"You are right, and I am sorry for it," James replied, turning his dark, handsome face toward her. "But since there have only been two topics of conversation since we arrived here, you may perhaps excuse me when my attention seems to wander."

"I assure you that your father should have been considerably annoyed to see you take such a strong line," Lady Woodstone went on with some asperity. "At least I know that *he* would never have gone against my wishes and insisted on shutting up the house in London in the middle of the Season!"

"Now, as to that, it is a matter of opinion," James said thoughtfully, "for I think that Father always wished to exercise a firmer hand, but found himself incapable of doing so."

"Because of his high regard for me!" his mother exclaimed.

"Just as you prefer," Lord Woodstone said in a faintly sardonic tone. "But, if you mean by that that I do not share his regard, as you put it, I think you are quite wrong."

"Do not think you can silence me by flattery," Lady Woodstone replied.

"I did not hope to do so, madam," James murmured, making a slight bow.

"I declare, you quite exasperate me!" his mother cried. "All of this because you fancy that your sister cannot conduct herself with decorum."

"I confess that decorum is scarcely the word which comes to mind when I think of Maria," James replied. "You are quite right in thinking that I would have left the house in Albemarle Street open and come down here alone had I thought that you could exercise sufficient control over her."

"Your efforts were no more successful than mine, sir," Lady Woodstone reminded him, drawing herself up like a ramrod. "And, besides, I think you were too particular by far. Surely it is only natural that a young lady should enjoy herself on the occasion of her coming out."

"Ah, but Maria would have made a bacchanalian festival of it, madam," her son replied, "and that would not have done at all. Perhaps next Season will find her more subdued."

"She should have been affianced *this* Season and not the next!" Lady Woodstone assured him, snipping a rose off with a pinch of her long fingers and flinging it to the ground in her impatience.

"May I take it from that that you would have approved of an alliance with a fop like Lord Webster?" James demanded. "I would not have thought to find you so well inclined toward someone who curls his hair with a hot iron and wears a patch shaped like a rooster."

"But of course there was no question of your sister accepting anyone like that," his mother protested, pausing in the shade of an arbor overspread with creepers, vines and roses.

"Lord Webster was quite the pick of the lot Maria preferred to surround herself with," James reminded her. "Do you remember the Marquess of Eldown who was always to be seen prancing about on high-heeled red shoes?"

"Your sister did not mean to seriously encourage that sort of person," Lady Woodstone said petulantly.

"Whatever her intent was, I do not pretend to know," her son replied, "but the effect was the same. Had I allowed her another fortnight in London, she would have succeeded in ruining her chances with any suitable young gentleman."

"Well, as for that, it is simply her high spirits," his mother muttered.

"Combined with a total lack of discrimination," James added grimly. "It is not that I care one way or another whether she marries wealth. Even a title is beside the point, but I feel that I owe it to Father, at least, to see that she does not marry a fool or worse."

"And so you have seen fit to surround her with nothing else but fools," Lady Woodstone replied sharply. "That was very astute of you, I'm sure."

"Come, Mother," James said, his face growing darker still in his annoyance. "You know as well as I do that Maria will find no gentlemen of the sort she dotes on here. And as for our neighbors being fools, I think you are quite wrong in that. Squire Eaton struck me as quite a sensible sort, and I am sure his daughter provided us with a more stimulating conversation than you are accustomed to in London."

"The chit seemed to think the doings of Napoleon might have been of some interest to me," his mother retorted. "Ladies should not concern themselves with politics, not to speak of military matters. And, as for her comments on the subject of the Prince Regent, I thought she demonstrated a complete lack of delicacy."

"I fancy that Miss Eaton is a young lady who speaks her mind," Lord Woodstone said firmly. "At least she conducted herself like a lady, which is more than can be said for my sister."

"Maria must make moon eyes at someone or she will die of boredom," his mother informed him. "Not that I was happy to see the way she wove a spell around that young dolt, but if you *must* provide her with no better company, why then she will amuse herself."

The hint of pride in his mother's voice did not escape Lord Woodstone's notice, for he had long since realized that, sharp-tongued and critical as his mother was with others, Maria's unexpected beauty made some amends for her own plainness, and it was with a degree of gratification that she saw her daughter able to turn heads in a manner she had never been able to do as a girl. It explained, he thought, the disturbing way in which she spoiled the girl and he thought, not for the first time, that she had set herself against attempting to change Maria's character since it suited her better than she would admit to be the mother of such a butterfly.

"Of course," Lady Woodstone said, "there must be limits, for although it is one thing for her to flirt with the squire's son in our own drawing room, there must be no question of her attending rustic entertainments. But I shall leave you the task of informing Maria of that. Since you have taken so much on yourself, you may as well prevent any further disappointments."

James glanced at her curiously. The dying light seemed to lengthen his face, raising his high cheekbones into prominence.

"I am afraid, madam, I do not know what you are referring to," he said.

"Surely I mentioned the invitation to some soirée or other in the village which I received the other day," his mother murmured. "Contra dancing in a town hall, I believe. So curious to think that anyone could believe that we might attend.

But then, perhaps, since I was gracious enough to receive the squire and his family . . ."

"I wish you would not condescend so much, madam," James said angrily. "This is the first I have heard of any such invitation, as well you know, and I am of the opinion that we should accept it. I, for one, would like to be on good terms with my neighbors and, if Miss Eaton is any example of the sort of young ladies one finds in the village, I think they might stand as a better model of propriety to Maria than most of the friends she made in London. I hope you have not sent a refusal yet."

Lady Woodstone glowered at him.

"Indeed, I did not think to make any response at all," she said bitterly. "Besides, if I remember correctly, the date was for Thursday next and that will make it quite impossible for us to attend since Lady Knightly would never think of exposing dear Drusella to such society."

"And what has Lady Knightly to do with us?" James demanded, turning to face his mother.

"Why, only that Althea is a fond enough friend to have agreed to mitigate my loneliness," Lady Woodstone said with a note of pathos in her voice.

"You cannot mean that you have invited her here!" James exclaimed.

"I knew you would not wish to separate me from her," Lady Woodstone said in what for her passed as a conciliatory tone. "After all, my dear, *I* am not the one being punished!"

"No one is being punished!" James said grimly. "But that is by the by. I take it that we are about to receive guests."

"They arrive tomorrow," his mother said with a note of triumph in her voice. "It is too late, I assure you, to put them off. Surely you will be glad enough to have Rupert at hand, for a more charming young man I have seldom met."

"Rupert's only charm lies in his inheritance," Lord Woodstone told her. "Aside from that he is as bumptious a fellow as I have ever met. And as for his sister, she is as witless as Maria."

"I will not have my friends spoken of in such a manner, sir!" his mother declared, raising the thin line of her nose to the sky. "I have bent enough in allowing you to exile us from London with very little protest, but I will not be kept entirely from polite Society. Besides, I am sure it was very good of Althea to take Drusella out of the city before the Season is over."

"You know as well as I do what Lady Knightly has in mind," James said dryly. "And I assure you that plot as you and she may, I will find Drusella no more attractive in the country than I did in London."

"That is as may be," his mother told him sharply. "There is still Rupert to consider. I have always hoped that he and Maria . . ."

"Surely you could not wish to see your daughter affianced to such a sapskull!" James exclaimed, thinking that he himself had been a fool

25

to think that he could thwart the plans of the lady who marched beside him.

"I see no use in continuing this discussion, sir," Lady Woodstone informed him. "They will arrive tomorrow and that, I think, is that!"

And, with those words, she proceeded into the house with the air of having passed some Rubicon of her own, leaving her son to stare grimly after her.

CHAPTER
Three

*S*usan Eaton made her second visit to Muir Hall under duress.

"I cannot think why Lady Woodstone should have invited us a second time," she told her mother in a low voice as Franklin guided the family gig along a particularly rutty stretch of road. "And why should she want us to meet her guests? I declare I would have refused to accompany you had I not wished to keep my eyes peeled."

And she nodded meaningfully at her brother who was flourishing the reins with abandon. A bright-eyed young man with a remarkably smooth face, Franklin Eaton was distinguished in no particular way except for the thick red hair which was not entirely hidden by the glossy black top hat which he had borrowed from his father, the squire having discovered that certain urgent matters prevented him from accompanying them on their afternoon call.

"I can only think that Lady Woodstone wishes to amuse herself by showing us off to her guests as an example of the general undesirability of country society," Susan continued, tossing her head.

"I would be obliged, my dear, if you did not work yourself into a pet," her mother said mildly. "And as for our being undesirable, that is great nonsense, I hope. Why, I'm sure you look as smart as any young lady they might have known in London. Green always did suit you."

Although the compliment did little to mollify Susan, she lapsed into silence, seeing that her mother, florid in her best burgundy silk with matching bonnet, was in no mood to review an argument which had been presented several times before. As for Franklin, a man of few words at any time, it was apparent that so caught up was he in some private vision of delight that any speculations on her part would go unheard.

Half an hour later found Susan with her suspicions vindicated, at least to her own satisfaction, since Lady Woodstone's cool, languid welcome had been followed by a condenscending acknowledgement of the existence of the Eatons on the part of her dear friend, Lady Knightly, an angular personage who wore the expression of one who constantly smells something singularly unpleasant.

As for Drusella Knightly, Susan thought she had never seen anyone so given to simpers and giggles. Plain to the point of ugliness, Lady Knightly's daughter was resplendent in pink and white taffeta with a bodice cut unfortunately low for one who possessed so many visible bones in quite unlikely places. Having extended two limp fingers in greeting, she retired to a corner from which she could be heard tittering at some private joke.

Sir Rupert, on the other hand, was far more enthusiastic than Susan thought quite proper, since, although he paid very little attention to her mother and brother, he seemed determined to keep by her side, ogling her in a manner which, in any other circumstance, she would have thought amusing.

Tea was served almost immediately and it did not escape Susan's notice that Lady Woodstone cleverly managed to arrange for herself and Lady Knightly to be seated some little distance from Mrs. Eaton with Drusella completing the circle. Maria, however, was not content to maintain a splendid isolation. Ignoring her mother's pointed request that she take a chair by her side, the golden-haired girl proceeded to lavish cakes and attention on a tongue-tied Franklin who gazed at her adoringly.

Thus, while the two ladyships chattered about London matters, making no attempt to include Mrs. Eaton in the conversation, Drusella simpered and giggled alternately, Maria fluttered her eyelashes, Franklin turned first red then white, and Sir Rupert muttered random remarks of which the most penetrating was that this was a 'dashed pretty countryside,' Susan concentrated on hiding her rising fury.

Lord Woodstone's arrival brought her a certain measure of relief since, after apologizing for having been delayed by his estate agent, he drew a chair up to her mother's side and began to question her about country matters, demonstrating so much apparent interest that Mrs. Eaton was soon chatting away quite happily.

Matters were not improved, however, when, the last cup of tea having been poured, Lady Woodstone suggested an entertainment.

"Drusella, my dear, you must play the pianoforte for us," she declared. "And Maria will sing."

"Delightful!" Lady Knightly exclaimed as the two girls took their positions. "What a treat this will be for all of us!"

No sooner had the first key been struck and the first high C trilled, however, than Susan realized that what she was being forced to endure was very far from a treat. It could only be said that both young ladies showed the same fine disregard for harmony and when it became clear that the recital was to be of a prolonged nature, Susan slipped from her chair and casually walked to one of the long windows which opened onto the garden, grateful that Sir Rupert had apparently slipped into a hypnotic state no doubt induced by repeated trials of this sort. The window being open, Susan could not resist the opportunity to escape, and soon found herself walking across the broad lawn, telling herself that if her absence should be noted she would make the excuse of having left feeling quite faint.

Such an apology was not necessary, however, when Lord Woodstone joined her.

"I cannot blame you for beating a retreat, Miss Eaton," he said. "I can only thank you for giving me the courage to do the same."

"But surely your mother will be annoyed," Susan replied. "She did not seem to note my departure, but I am certain that she will have noticed yours."

"Why, as for that," he said, smiling, "I am no stranger to her disapproval. Indeed, I think it is I who will show some annoyance when she and I meet privately, for I do not think she has been as warm a hostess as I dared—no doubt foolishly—to hope she would be when I suggested that she invite you and your mother and brother here again."

There was a stone sundial nearby, overgrown with moss yet still sporting the time-honored inscription *memento mori*, and here Susan made pause to look up at Lord Woodstone curiously.

"I wondered that it could have been Her Ladyship's idea," she said in a low voice, "since she has not seen fit to return our first call."

"I fear my mother is a snob of the first water," he assured her dryly. "It is, I assure you, some comfort to me that that is the worst of her faults."

"You will satisfy my curiosity, sir," Susan replied, "if you would explain precisely why you wished her to receive us again, particularly when she has her fine friends to amuse her."

For a moment Lord Woodstone was silent. A cloud passed over the sun and his face at one and the same moment. In the distance Drusella could be heard striking discord after discord while Maria trilled a melody which seemed to have very little to with the tune being played.

"I can be frank, I hope," he said finally.

"I would like it best of all things," Susan assured him.

"I guessed that straightforwardness would be your forte, Miss Eaton," he said with some satisfaction, although his dark eyes remained hooded. "Very well, then, I wished you to call again in the hopes that my sister, at least, could make some comparison between Lady Knightly and her unfortunate daughter and you and your mother."

"And for what purpose, pray?" Susan replied, determined not to be charmed by what seemed to be an indirect compliment.

"Maria has been provided with very uncertain examples of decorum," he explained in a troubled voice. "No doubt you were startled by her behavior on your first visit."

"She seems to be a—a lively person," Susan hedged, taken by surprise at the directness with which he had come to the point.

"Not to put too fine a point on it," Lord Woodstone told her, "my sister is an incorrigible flirt. In London she made such a show of herself that I was forced to insist on this remove to the country, although, under any other circumstances, I would have come down here alone and left her to our mother."

Since there did not seem to be anything for Susan to say, she remained silent.

"The visit of Lady Knightly and her family has come as an unhappy surprise to me," Lord Woodstone continued. "Drusella will teach my sister little that she should know and a great deal that she should not. Let me be direct. I had hoped that Maria might become your friend."

"Why, as to that," Susan told him, "I am not certain that she is aware of my existence."

"Ah, yes. Your brother!" Lord Woodstone exclaimed. "That is always the way of it. But then, he seems a sensible enough fellow, quite absorbed in his study of astronomy. Granted that he might provide the lure, but in the long run she will come to know you better and, perhaps, if you are willing to advise her, learn something of a ladylike reticence she does not possess at the present."

"You are suggesting that I should become her tutor, sir," Susan said, making no attempt to hide her astonishment.

"It is a great deal to ask, I know," Lord Woodstone said, turning his dark eyes on her. "And I would quite understand if you should refuse. Maria is a trial to one's patience. I confess."

"It is not my patience that I am concerned with, sir," Susan told him.

"What else, then?" he asked intently. "Once you come to know her better, you will discover that she is delightful in many ways. Particularly when taken separately from my mother."

"It is not that," Susan assured him. "I would willingly be your sister's friend were it not for the fact that . . ."

"I have been frank, Miss Eaton, and so must you," Lord Woodstone encouraged her.

"Very well, then," Susan said. "The fact is that, although my brother's obsession with astronomy usually causes him to be impervious to the attractions of the female gender both in general and in particular, in this case . . ."

"Surely you do not mean that he has taken Maria seriously!" Lord Woodstone exclaimed.

"But that is precisely what I *do* mean, sir," Susan told him. "Given those conditions, I am certain that you will understand why it is impossible for me to encourage your sister to see a great deal of me, even if your mother would agree."

"Why, that is an unfortunate turn of events," Lord Woodstone muttered. "You must accept my apologies again, Miss Eaton, for I would not for the world be implicated in any arrangement which might lead to your brother's disappointment."

"I am glad to hear that," Susan said in a low

voice. "But I fear that does not solve the problem."

"What! Does he intend to declare for her, then?"

"I believe he does," Susan said, "as soon, no doubt, as he has occasion to be alone with her even for a moment."

"Then we must see that such an occasion does not present itself," Lord Woodstone told her. "Come now, Miss Eaton. Do not look so distressed. There is a way out of this, I'm sure."

"If there is I do not see it," Susan replied. "Unless, of course, you can persuade your sister not to lead him on."

"*I* can persuade her of nothing," Lord Woodstone declared. But there is this. Your brother, as I said, seems a sensible sort."

"I suppose he is, in his own fashion," Susan murmured. "But in this case I think he has transferred his obsession with astronomy to your sister and, in that case, I do not think we can look to him for any special show of common sense."

"We can hope for this, at least," Lord Woodstone replied. "If we can only keep him from proposing for a little while, he will have time to see my sister for what she is. At this very moment, for example, she may be casting sheep's eyes in Sir Rupert's direction. And at the village ball next Thursday . . ."

"Surely you do not intend to come!" Susan cried in dismay.

"At the village ball she will flit about like a

butterfly," Lord Woodstone said, so intent on his own thoughts that he did not notice her exclamation. "Yes. With that in mind I will run roughshod over my mother's objections. But listen. I believe the recital must be over."

"Then we must make a quick return," Susan assured him. "But think well as to what you have proposed, sir. I do not wish to sound unkind, but it might be as well if you did not mingle too intimately with your neighbors. They are simple people. Certain hopes may be raised. But I cannot speak more clearly."

"Then I will expect a more explicit explanation next time we meet, Miss Eaton," Lord Woodstone declared. "Until then you will understand, I'm sure, that I must follow my best judgement. But come. Let me take your arm. With luck we will not have been missed."

CHAPTER
Four

"*I declare, my dear, I* believe everyone in the village is here."

"Not the butcher, surely, Martha."

"You know as well as I do, Willamena, that the committee decided that anyone who could afford the guinea subscription would be quite welcome."

The first Miss Reardon's boney nose twitched in irritation.

"I spoke out at the time against it, Martha," she told her sister. "Only fancy attending a soirée with one's own maid!"

"We were not to know that she had saved the money," the second Miss Reardon reminded her. "And when it comes to that, I think that Patience looks most attractive."

"As well she should, considering that I took the trouble of lending her my third-best pearls."

"And I provided the lace fichu."

"Still, it does seem scarcely proper . . ."

Susan raised her handkerchief to her lips to suppress a smile. The Misses Reardon were favorites of hers, two elderly sisters whose only claim to fame rested in the fact that their father had been a general in His Majesty's forces. Their entire life having been spent in the ivy-covered brick house which faced the village green, they were so familiar with the various affairs of the village that they could, with very little hesitation, tell you to the hour when Mrs. Humber, the greengrocer's wife, had given birth to her daughter Molly ten years before. Furthermore, they were not averse to making speculation as to the future, having successfully predicted the drought of '87 and the accident which caused the wheelwright, John Chambers, to lose a finger in '92. As for their maid Patience, she was a pert young thing who succeeded in doing precisely as she pleased, the Reardon sisters being glad enough to show indulgence to someone who showed such a definite flair for collecting gossip.

"I believe it is an excellent thing that Patience has been allowed a bit of pleasure, even if it does mean that she mingles with her betters," Parson Dawson said in his pedantic manner, wagging his white head back and forth in his usual pendulum fashion, a habit which produced a sense of dizziness in his congregation when he spoke from the pulpit.

"But are we really her 'betters,' Papa?" his daughter Jane teased him. "For my own part I think Patience one of the cleverest people I know, for she told me herself that she could earn as many half crowns as she liked simply by keeping her ears open."

Susan smiled as she saw that her friend's words had brought a flush to both of the Misses Reardon's faces. Dressed in identical gowns of puce chintz, with identical lace caps set on grizzled curls, they turned to survey one another questioningly, mouths a bit ajar as always in order to accommodate their large and healthy teeth.

"Can it be that you have bribed the girl, Martha," the first Miss Reardon exclaimed.

"If she receives half crowns, Willamena, they could only come from you," her sister replied, "since I restrict myself to shillings."

"Then that was how you came to know that young Lucy Fowles was expecting even before she told her husband?" the first Miss Reardon cried.

"And this explains how it was you knew the Steptoe lad was off to join the army!"

Jane put her arm around Susan's waist and drew her to one side as accusations were hurled back and forth from sister to sister while their little maid, her subscription paid, joined the butcher's son in forming the line for the first cotillion.

"How wonderful it is to see your brother in attendance," Jane said gaily. "Tell me, Susan, how did you persuade him to separate from his telescope on such a clear night as this?"

Susan looked at her friend ruefully. No one could call Jane beautiful, to be sure, but her features were appealing enough with her short, turned-up nose and her blue eyes which sparkled like pools of water caught in sunlight. It was no secret that Jane Dawson's fancy had settled on Franklin Eaton when she was little more than a girl, although the gentleman in question remained oblivious to that fact, persisting in treating her like a sister. For years Susan had been convinced that the day would come when her brother would come quite literally to his sense and reciprocate Jane's affection. But now she realized that happy day was not to be, a fact of which her friend remained in total ignorance.

How she wished that she had had the time and words to explain precisely to Lord Woodstone why he and the party from Muir Hall should not attend this village dance. Such incalculable damage might be done as she could scarcely imagine. As it was, Franklin was lingering about the entrance of the hall, his eyes glazed with expectations. Jane was waiting for an answer to her question with a puzzled expression in her eyes which would soon, no doubt, be replaced by hurt and confusion. Across the room, Mrs. Jackson and her two daughters, Ruth and Priscilla, of whom the best that could be said was that neither was in the first flush of youth, waited with ill-concealed impatience for their first glimpse of the much heralded Lord Woodstone. Indeed the general attitude of expectation was so great that Susan could not bear to think of the effect which Lady Woodstone's and Lady Knightly's pointed air of condescension would have. She could only hope that they would arrive late and depart early, leaving behind as little disappointment and hurt as possible.

But, in the meantime, she must decide whether or not to warn Jane of the effect Maria Woodstone had made on Franklin, or whether to wait and hope that in the course of the past few days Sir Rupert might have attracted the girl's attention.

And then, quite suddenly, the decision was taken out of her hands by the arrival of the party from Muir Hall. The first to enter the small but festively decorated room with its platform to accommodate the fiddlers was Lady Woodstone, wearing a pale gray gown of such an elegant cut that one knew at once that no expense had been spared. Her Ladyship's fading brown hair had been elaborately dressed and decorated with an ostrich feather, all of which, together with the diamonds which sparkled at her neck, produced a general effect which made every other woman in the room feel just a bit shabby—which was,

Susan thought, no doubt Lady Woodstone's intention.

Lady Knightly followed, equally furbished, on Sir Rupert's arm. Casting one glance around the room with the expression of someone who has accidentally strayed into a fish market, she followed Lady Woodstone's lead to an unoccupied corner as far as possible from the rest of the assembly. Having settled themselves, the two ladies began what appeared to be an animated conversation, keeping their fans between their faces and the rest of the room in a way which could not have been better calculated to convey the message that they did not care to be disturbed.

Drusella was the next to make her appearance. Since the arrival of the gentry had put a temporary halt to lining for the cotillion, and even the fiddlers had broken off their tuning up, Drusella's first words were completely audible to all.

"I declare," she said to no one in particular, "what a pokey little room!"

And with that she flounced off to join her mother and Lady Woodstone.

The attention of the company was now focused on Maria Woodstone, a vision of delight in buttercup yellow. Franklin rushed forward, managing somehow to trip over his own feet in a manner which would have sent him sprawling to the floor had Lord Woodstone, who was directly behind his sister, not stepped forward and kept him upright. Undeterred, Franklin bowed to

Maria with such a thrust of the upper part of his body that it was necessary for Lord Woodstone to steady him again. Susan felt the hot blood rise in her cheeks as Maria flung her golden head back and laughed delightedly. But the next moment she was allowing the young man to lead her into the cotillion line with her usual lavish display of sunny smiles which she dispensed at random.

Susan heard Jane take a deep breath and turned to find her friend quite pale, an incredulous expression in her fine eyes.

"It will be all right," Susan said, trying to sound as though she was convinced of what she was saying. "Come, sit down. Mama will have brought her vinaigrette. That will soon put you right."

But Jane brushed the proposal of a restorative aside, although, Susan noted, she took the precaustion of sinking down onto a chair.

"You knew?" she said in a low voice which held a degree of accusation. "Come, confess. I can tell by looking at you that it came as no surprise. You should have told me, you know. Indeed you should. What a fool I have been all evening, congratulating myself on my new taffeta and expecting Franklin to ask me to join him on the dance floor at any moment. Why, shall I tell you something, Susan Eaton? I was addlepated enough to think that your brother attended tonight because—because he knew I should be here! Pray laugh if you like. What a cake I have made of myself, to be sure!"

It was clear to Susan that in the course of delivering this sotto-voiced speech, her friend's surprise and disappointment had been miraculously transformed into self-mockery and outrage, a combination which she sensed was of an explosive nature.

"Of course I have no one but myself to blame," Jane went on, staring straight in front of her, hands clasped on her lap. To anyone who could not hear her, she might have been discussing the music.

"But Jane . . ." Susan began.

"For years I have been mooning about your brother, waiting for the day to come when he would suddenly look at me—really look at me—and see that he had loved me all along."

Jane laughed sardonically.

"Well," she concluded. "It appears he has taken time from his books and telescope and nasty charts to look about him, at last, and I will not deceive myself by thinking that if I had been there rather than Miss Woodstone . . ."

She broke off and, turning her head, began to dab quickly at her eyes with a lace handkerchief.

"Oh, Jane!" Susan exclaimed, sitting down beside her and taking her hands. "I can see now I should have warned you, but believe me when I say that I did not think the company from Muir Hall would actually condescend to rub shoulders with the hoi polloi."

"You were only concerned about my *seeing* how he adores her!" Jane exclaimed. "What sort of answer is that, pray? Surely I have been constant enough to have deserved to be told at any rate, since obviously he means to offer for her."

"And do you think it possible someone like Maria Woodstone would accept?" Susan said in a low voice.

"In the ordinary way of things, no," Jane replied, her brown eyes flashing to where Franklin and the lady in question were cavorting about the room. "However, it is plain as plain can be that she is completely infatuated with him."

"Listen to me, Jane," Susan said with sudden urgency. "You must believe me when I tell you that I have it on the best authority that Miss Woodstone is a compulsive flirt. Her fancy strays wherever there is a new and interesting gentleman to be found, and she always follows it."

Jane assumed a dubious expression which Susan, watching the apparently adoring glances which Maria was casting Franklin as she passed him in the line, could quite understand. But there was no opportunity to continue her explanation, for quite suddenly Sir Rupert was standing before her, his white cravat arranged in such an extraordinarily elaborate manner that it could be nothing but the latest fashion. Under the long bangs of his Brutus cut, his eyes fixed on her in the determined way she remembered all too well.

Without showing any undue enthusiasm

which, indeed, she did not feel, Susan introduced him to her friend, but it was apparent that no one else interested him, as he made manifestly clear by the casual bow which he made Jane, who responded by murmuring something unintelligible and hurrying off to join her father.

Taking a deep breath, Susan submitted to a conversation which was very like the one Sir Rupert had engaged her in at Muir Hall. Dutifully she agreed that the assembly hall was 'dashed quaint,' the company 'havey-cavey'—whatever that might mean—and that it was a 'curst nuisance' that the evening was so warm. With these important matters settled, Sir Rupert seemed to be at a loss as to what else to say until, the music for the cotillion having scraped to an end, he asked her for the next dance.

Above all, Susan did not wish to take the floor with him, if for no better reason that, in so doing she would appear to Jane to have cast her lot with the Muir Hall company. She was searching her mind for some excuse, at the same time keeping one eye on Maria who having attached herself to Franklin like a limpet, was leading him toward Lady Woodstone, when Lord Woodstone joined Sir Rupert by her side.

"You see, Miss Eaton," he said with a slow smile, "I have been as good as my word."

"I wish you had been less faithful to it, sir," Susan said with some asperity.

"You said you would explain your peculiar point of view to me at our next meeting," Lord

Woodstone said in a low voice, his dark eyes hooded. "Perhaps if we were to stroll about the room . . ."

"Miss Eaton is engaged to me for the next dance, old chap," Sir Rupert interrupted. "With that in mind, I'd be obliged if you would cut the line, eh?"

"I am afraid you have misunderstood me, sir," Susan said promptly, "since I have decided not to take the floor this evening. And, as for your offer, my lord, I will be happy to accept it on condition that you allow me to introduce you to my friends, not a few of whom would be delighted to dance with you, I'm sure."

It was a challenge which she was certain that he understood, for his dark eyes glittered with amusement as he extended his arm.

"If that is the price I must pay for an explanation, Miss Eaton, I accept with pleasure," Lord Woodstone said.

"Very well, sir," Susan said as they began their slow progress, leaving Sir Rupert staring balefully after them. "I am particularly interested in having you meet Mrs. Jackson and her two daughters."

CHAPTER
Five

The next morning
found Jane Dawson closeted with Susan in the
back sitting room of the Eaton's square brick
house on the outskirts of the village. Despite the
lateness of the hour that both girls had retired
the night before, they displayed the natural vivac-
ity of young ladies who had a great deal of a
confidential nature to discuss.

"Would you believe," Jane said before she had
as much as seated herself, "that Ruth and Priscilla Jackson are already arguing over which one
of them Lord Woodstone prefers! I declare that
when I met them coming out of the greengrocer's
not ten minutes ago, they were so busy making
their arguments that they did not even notice
me."

"I expect you will blame me for that," Susan

said sadly, "since I was the one who introduced him to them."

Jane shook her brown curls. "They would have been crushed if you had not done so," she assured her friend, "and it was good of him to dance with each of them, I'm sure, especially when Ruth insisted on continuing to crack him on the shoulder with her fan."

"That was only because she was nervous, poor dear," Susan reflected. "Why, I cannot recollect the last time she took the floor with anyone."

"Still, it was handsome of him to keep his face quite straight even when Priscilla persisted in braying like a donkey at every word he said."

"Oh, Lord Woodstone can be charming, I'm sure," Susan declared. "Particularly when he wants something."

"But surely the Jackson sisters had nothing to offer him except a few awkward moments," Jane protested.

"I mean by that that he danced with them because I made it one condition which must be fulfilled before I would talk to him seriously on a matter which concerns me," Susan told her. "But now I think that I was wrong. It would have been better had he shown his true colors by ignoring them, as he would have done under any other circumstance. Now he has raised their hopes and made them quarrel with one another, and I cannot congratulate myself for that, I think."

"Do you mean to say that you bargained with

him to be personable?" Jane asked her, puzzled. "But on what basis, pray?"

"Only that I had warned him on the occasion of my last visit to Muir Hall that it would be better if he and his company did not make themselves too familiar with the village. There was no time then to explain, but I promised to satisfy his curiosity later. And so I did."

"That must have been over supper," Jane said wisely, "for I saw the two of you thick as thieves. And I was not the only one who noticed, I assure you."

"I made no effort to make a secret of it," Susan said, sitting very stiff and straight in her sprigged muslin and lace fichu, which costume should have made her seem demure but somehow failed.

"What did you tell him, pray?" Jane demanded. "Whatever it was, I could see he was not pleased."

"As for that, I can take no responsibility," Susan said stoutly, "for he should have known that no good would come of mixing wine with water."

"I hope you spoke more plainly to him than that," her friend replied, "although I suppose you mean that the Quality should not mix with the hoi polloi."

"It may not always follow," Susan told her, "but in this case I am certain that it does. What have we but a young gentleman with any amount of wealth at his command who wishes to play at

51

being farmer? Add to that a mother who is so proud that it is a wonder her nose does not stick to the ceiling of every room she enters. Add to that a flitter-gibbet of a sister who plays wild and loose with the heart of anyone who has the ill fortune to wear Hessian boots, with no more thought of the consequences than my pet tabby."

"Susan!" Jane exclaimed.

"I cannot help it if I am angry," her friend told her, "and if I were you I would make a stronger comparison than that, I assure you!"

"But surely you did not put it to Lord Woodstone in precisely that manner!"

"I was delicate enough to please the Misses Reardon," Susan assured her. "But I did not put too fine a point on it. What good had it done, I asked him, to travel up from Muir Hall with his little company in order that all of them, except his sister, should sit and sneer, or, in the case of Sir Rupert, lounge in corners and stare through his quizzing glass in much the same manner one observes a—a bear baiting."

"And what did Lord Woodstone say to that?" Jane exclaimed, her blue eyes sparkling. It was not the first time she had had reason to marvel at Susan's directness of approach.

"Why, at first he laughed," her friend replied, "but then he saw that I was quite serious. There was no need for me to mention his sister's behavior, given the fact that she and Franklin were sitting opposite us and she was feeding him tidbits of cold salmon like a pet dog."

Jane appeared to be torn between amusement and the painful memory which she herself held of the same scene. But, being a young lady of essentially good humor, she turned herself to a consideration of the comparisons which had been made.

"I declare I cannot blame Lord Woodstone for laughing," she said. "Think of the images you conjured up. Sir Rupert watching a bear baiting through his quizzing glass—and who can think of anyone feeding cold salmon to a dog?"

"Perhaps those were not the precise words I used," Susan told her, "although since I was quite beside myself with anger, I cannot be certain."

"Besides," Jane continued, serious now, "I do not like to think of your brother in that manner. It was not kind of you say anything of the sort, Susan."

"Franklin has lost my patience, as well," Susan declared. "I tried to speak quite plainly to him on our return home, but you know what he is. I do not think he heard a word I said."

Jane clenched her hands and stared at the pattern on the carpet.

"When a gentleman is in love . . ." she began and then lapsed into silence.

"Love!" Susan exclaimed. "Why, it is nothing of the sort, I assure you. He is besotted! I can think of no better word to describe it. Why, I am ashamed to think of the way he acted. Even

Papa was put out, I believe, although he did not say a word."

"No doubt he thinks he has no right to interfere," Jane said sadly. "After all, your brother is of age and your father has always let him follow his own course."

"Staring through a telescope for hours at an end is one thing," Susan assured her, "and letting oneself be played like a puppet is another. It will come to nothing, you understand. That is what I wanted to tell you last night when Sir Rupert interrupted us. Lord Woodstone himself assured me that his sister flits from gentleman to gentleman like a butterfly."

"Even butterflies light sometimes," Jane said in a low voice. "You cannot be certain that Miss Woodstone is not serious in this case."

"Even if she were," Susan said flushing, "do you think her mother would allow anything to come of it? She was forced to come down here to the country quite against her will and you saw for yourself how she and Lady Knightly behaved. Why, when I think of the way in which they ignored everyone, I swear I think my blood begins to boil."

"If you went on like this to Lord Woodstone, I can well see why he ceased to be amused," Jane said thoughtfully. "Do you think that you were wise?"

"I think I only went too far when I suggested that he was only interested in my opinion because he wants to rent the north meadow from Papa," Susan said in a low voice.

"You *did* not!"

"I am afraid I did," Susan replied, her face quite rosy now. "It was shortly after that he and his company left."

"I should have thought they might!" Jane exclaimed. "But come! Do you think so poorly of the gentleman?"

"I cannot tell," Susan replied. "I only know that although he agreed with me that, once at Muir Hall, his sister should be kept a far distance from Franklin, he persisted in bringing her to the dance. That in itself makes me doubt his sincerity; although, of course, he would have it that if my brother was given opportunity enough to observe the lady in question he would soon see that she is far from being sincere."

"He cannot have advocated both measures simultaneously," Jane protested. "To keep her at a distance and, at the same time, allow Franklin to observe . . ."

"I should not have put it quite that way," Susan interrupted her. "Our first agreement was that my brother should have no opportunity of being *alone* with his sister in order that a proposal might be made. Perhaps, to do him credit, he may have thought that there might have been some other gentleman at the entertainment last night who would attract her attention, which only goes to show how little he knows of Thrumhill. And *that*," she concluded breathlessly, "was the point I tried to make. He should not experiment with people's happiness."

"I think . . ." Jane began hesitantly.

"Do go on," Susan begged her. "For you know how I value your opinion."

"I think that in your eagerness to see your brother safe, you may have been unfair to Lord Woodstone," Jane declared. "I have no more good words than you to say for his mother or his sister, not to mention Lady Knightly and her peculiar daughter, but I think that, on the whole, Lord Woodstone did his best to make himself agreeable. There was no need for him to allow the Misses Reardon to occupy him for nearly a half hour in conversation. Even your father's north meadow does not carry that value, I believe."

"There is no need for irony," Susan protested.

"Then let me put it this way. You were dancing with Sir Rupert at the time . . ."

"Only because he *would* press me until I thought I would scream."

"That's as may be, but I was sitting close by and I heard the questions they put to Lord Woodstone. Why, given a few more minutes they would have had his family history complete."

"He made himself agreeable to them, then?" Susan said with a quaver of uncertainty in her voice.

"No one could have been more charming," Jane assured her. "And he spoke at length with my father on conditions in the parish."

"He is only playing at being lord of the manor," Susan muttered.

"Indeed I think he wants to like and be liked," her friend told her. "Be fair, Susan, if you can. It is no fault of his how his mother and sister behave. Not to mention his guests. You must admit it was Lord Woodstone who rescued you from Sir Rupert."

"I did not say he had a heart of stone," Susan replied. "I dare say he is quite prepared to be kind. But I, for one, do not want his charity."

Jane looked at her thoughtfully.

"And do you think," she said, "that in waging a private war with Lord Woodstone you will do most to protect Franklin?"

Susan opened her mouth to speak, but no words came, and in the next moment the door to the sitting room opened and Franklin himself made his appearance, progressing with a measured tread like a sleepwalker. It was only when he had succeeded in stepping on Susan's toe with one foot and crushing Jane's reticule, which had slipped to the floor, with the other that he made some note of their existence.

"Do sit down, Franklin!" Susan said impatiently. "I should like to have a little talk with you."

"In that event I think I will be going," Jane said hastily, gathering her skirts about her as she rose.

But, although he graced his sister and her

guest with a vague smile, Franklin made no pause and had soon passed into the front parlor.

"When he awakens," Susan said grimly, "it will be with a rude shock indeed. Oh, Jane, can you blame me for wanting to protect him?"

"You know my feelings," Jane said, embracing her. "I would protect him myself if it were in my power. But have a care, my dear, to be fair to everyone, and not the least to yourself."

CHAPTER
Six

Thin strips of bread and butter, together with sponge biscuits were all the refreshments provided by the Misses Reardon at their famous card parties on Tuesday evenings, but for all that, no one in the village had ever been known to refuse an invitation unless he or she were grappling with a dire emergency, if for no other reason than that the best way to avoid being the subject of gossip was to be in attendance. For some there was also the added fillip of enjoying the hospitality of what came as close as anything the village could provide to real gentry, the spinsters' father having been a general in His Majesty's forces.

Mrs. Eaton attended, however, not for any of these motives, but because she was extraordinarily fond of whist or, as she liked to put it, her 'little weakness,' and thus it was, since Susan was always included in the invitation as a matter of course, she found herself, on the first Tuesday evening following the dance, in the Misses Reardon's cozy parlor with a fire burning in the hearth and three card tables, each covered with their green baize tops and set with candles and fresh packs of cards.

Patience, neat and tidy in her blue and white uniform, attended the door through which Susan and her mother were followed by Parson Dawson and Jane, Mrs. Jackson accompanied by Ruth and Priscilla wearing beribboned gowns which some might say were better suited to young ladies in their first flush of youth; Captain Blazemore, the village bachelor, and Mr. Lawson, the village schoolmaster and his wife, the former Miss Acton from Springwell, a sprightly lady who had never once in the thirty years of her marriage ceased to thank her good fortune for the rise she had had in the world.

The serious business of refreshment having first to be settled, Patience saw to the setting of a tea tray on each table and for the next fifteen minutes little was heard in the room beside the spitting of the fire and the rattle of delicate china. Once this small ceremony had been consummated, however, it was with some eagerness that the cards were cut and the game begun, Parson Dawson having made his usual feeble protest to the threepenny points which the others insisted gave more relish to the play.

But the high point of the evening began, as it always did, promptly at nine when the trays appeared again, this time bearing the burden of wine and biscuits, and conversation turned from the taking of tricks to more general matters. Miss Martha Reardon, as was customary, took the lead.

"How fortunate we are, I think," she said in her fine, thread-thin voice, "to have the lights shining at Muir Hall again."

"La, Sister, what a one for skirting the subject you are!" the first Miss Reardon exclaimed. "Lights shining, indeed. Why, if they are I am sure neither you nor I have seen them or are likely to as far as Lady Woodstone is concerned."

" 'Twas just a manner of speaking, Willamena," the second Miss Reardon replied with her usual energy. "And although Lady Woodstone may be hoity-toity enough, her son is a charming young fellow, unless I am much mistaken."

At that she paused and looked about the room in the manner of one who would like nothing better than to be challenged. And, although Susan could have done so, she held her tongue.

The fact of the matter was that she was in no mood to argue with anyone. Indeed she would have been absent tonight had her mother not made it quite so clear that unless she made an appearance they would be one player short for three tables. The last time such a catastrophe had occurred, she reminded her daughter, it had

61

been necessary for their hostesses to press Patience to make up one of the foursomes with unfortunate results, since it appeared that the little maid's cleverness was sufficient to make her the winner, hands down, and the evening had ended with her apron pocket bulging to quite awkward proportions.

However, even though Susan had been present in the flesh, her thoughts had been distracted from the game, for, as though it had not been enough to have been reprimanded by Jane, she had had no better luck in convincing her father that drastic steps should be taken to prevent Franklin from ever setting eyes on Maria Woodstone again.

"As for sending the lad away," he had countered when she had made the suggestion, "it is only reasonable that he cannot take a holiday from a holiday. He does as little here as he could do anywhere else. And there is no question of my sending him off to conduct my business elsewhere, even if there was any to be had, since he knows as little of my affairs as it is possible for any single person not to know. Besides, if, as you say, the girl has no serious intentions, he will only get his fingers burned, which, to my thinking, might do him a bit of good. Why, it has been my experience that there's nothing like a bit of disappointment now and then to make a fellow appreciate what he has. Teach him to value peace of mind, eh?"

Seeing that there was nothing to be gained

from that quarter, Susan had taken herself to her brother's study and, having forced his attention with some considerable effort, made her points clearly from first to last, whereupon Franklin had indicated in an equally blunt fashion that she knew very little of Miss Woodstone's nature. He had then gone on to recite that lady's virtues in such a prolonged and monotonous fashion, much as he had been accustomed to speak of astronomy in the past, that despite her urgent interest in the matter, Susan had found herself nodding off from sheer boredom, and had finally left him alone with his monologue convinced that nothing she could do or say would persuade Franklin that his high hopes were doomed to be shattered. Indeed she had been brought to wonder why she attempted to protect him and was forced to revert to her determination that the family pride should not be lessened through his bull-headedness.

But even these dismal thoughts could not hold her captive when Lord Woodstone's name continued to be bandied about with such enthusiasm.

"Such a delightful sense of humor!" Miss Ruth Jackson trilled, patting the little row of black curls which hid the graying hair beneath.

"So up-to-date on all the latest opinions!" her sister declared.

"I declare I do not think I have ever seen a young gentleman so perfectly—so perfectly suited," their mother agreed.

There was, Susan noted, no need for anyone

in the company to ask her for what Lord Woodstone seemed to be suited.

"Of course, Susan knows him best," the first Miss Reardon said coyly, fluttering her fan.

"Tell us your impressions, my dear," her sister urged.

Susan flushed, feeling every eye in the room on her.

"I'm sure he's a pleasant enough gentleman," she said in a low voice, "although I think we make a great mistake if we think that any one of us can engage more than his passing interest."

"A falling out already!" the second Miss Reardon whispered to her sister.

"I would not have thought they knew one another well enough as yet," Miss Willamena replied.

"Perhaps you would do better to consider his mother," Susan declared, furious at having been so deliberately misunderstood and intent, above all else, in turning the conversation.

"Not a very pleasant woman, I think," Mrs. Eaton ventured.

"No doubt she and her friend were feeling a bit awkward, my dear," her husband remonstrated, being an ardent admirer of the aristocracy.

"Indeed, I think we must be generous," Parson Dawson added in his usual gentle voice. "First impressions are frequently misleading, I have found."

"Still, Lady Knightly's daughter *did* appear to

spend the entire evening laughing at us," Mrs. Eaton declared, ignoring her husband's warning glance. "Either that or she is a victim of some curious malaise."

"I find it more likely that she is simple," the first Miss Reardon said firmly. "Indeed my sister and I both noted a certain vacant expression about the eyes."

"Perhaps that *is* the kindest speculation," Parson Dawson ventured, shifting restlessly in his chair, for though he was an ardent devotee of whist, he often found it difficult to reconcile the nature of the conversation which followed with his role as village peacemaker. Although, as he often told his daughter, perhaps it was as well that he was on hand each Tuesday to hear the worst that was being said, first hand.

However, much to Susan's frustration, on this occasion, with the exception of Drusella, the company at Muir Hall was let off more gently than she had hoped. True, Miss Martha Reardon made a few abrasive comments concerning the conduct of Miss Maria Woodstone, only however to be reminded by her sister that the young lady was fresh from London and could not be expected to behave in the local manner.

"And, besides, Franklin seemed in such fine form I doubt that she could help herself," she added with a sly glance in Mrs. Eaton's direction.

At that, Susan found herself bristling, as much on Jane's account as any other, but before she could speak her friend had turned the conversation to Sir Rupert, whereupon both the Misses Reardon's steely black eyes began to sparkle.

"A fine looking fellow, I thought," Miss Martha said, her eyes intent on Susan's face.

"Not a great one with words, I think," Miss Willamena added.

"It that was the fellow with the extraordinary cravat," Captain Blazemore declared, making his first contribution to the conversation having been intent up to this point on diminishing the contents of the brandy decanter, "I would not trust him as far as a sparrow can hop, and that's the honest truth."

Captain Blazemore's rare assessments of character being well listened to, thanks to what the Misses Reardon primly referred to as his 'worldly' background, the company waited expectantly. But it was clear that he intended to say no more, contenting himself with wagging his grizzled head backward and forward in the manner of one who has indulged himself too well.

"Well, I am very sorry to hear that, I'm sure," Miss Martha Reardon said in a tone which seemed to prove that just the opposite was true. "Very sorry, indeed. But then, a word to the wise never did anyone any harm, as I think you'll agree, Susan."

"I am afraid I do not take your meaning," Susan confessed. "Unless it is because I took the floor with him for a single cotillion."

"Ah, but then of course there was his call on

Monday," Miss Willamena said in her most sprightly manner.

"His call?" Susan exclaimed, truly bewildered.

"I am afraid you must be mistaken," her mother told her hostess, "for we spent Monday marketing in Dunhill and the squire was out of the house all day."

"But surely he left his card with Betty," Miss Martha protested.

"You know as well as I do, Sister, that Patience told us that Betty was off walking with young Tom Thomas at the time," Miss Willamena expostulated.

Susan saw Jane bite her lip and wondered what she found so amusing.

"You are fortunate in Patience's sharp eyes," she said, rising. "As for Sir Rupert calling at our house, I cannot think that he was motivated by anything more than boredom. And now, Mama, I think we must take our leave."

Parson Dawson and Jane accompanied them, but the others remained behind, Captain Blazemore to nurse his glass, and the others to lend their eager ears. Or so Susan thought, since as Patience opened the door for them she heard Miss Martha say something about a sly puss, while her sister added that, in her opinion, there was no better way to attract the attention of one gentleman than by attracting the attention of another. As a consequence, it was with considerable bad humor that Susan, having taken leave of Jane and her father by the gate, strode home at such a pace that poor Mrs. Eaton was left quite breathless in trying to keep up with her.

"They *will* see everything as they care to see it!" the girl exclaimed, having reached the privacy of her own chamber. "But if I am the only one to remain clear-eyed, then it follows that Franklin will be my responsibility entirely."

CHAPTER
Seven

*S*quire Eaton was a patient man, well noted in the village for his common sense and honesty of purpose. His reluctance to discuss the matter of his son's infatuation with Susan stemmed, as a consequence, not from any desire to avoid the facts, but rather from his firm conviction that anything which could rouse Franklin from his obsession with amateur astronomy might not have entirely unfortunate results.

Indeed the squire had thought long and hard on the matter, even though it was clear to him as it was to Susan that Miss Maria Woodstone would never hesitate to break his son's heart with her carefree airs. However, it had also occurred to him that this might result in awakening Franklin to the practicalities of life, with the possible result that the young man might decide to take some passing interest, at least, in his father's affairs. Not only that eventuality must be considered, as the squire had told his wife in the privacy of their bedchamber—but once his heart was broken Franklin might see fit to mend it by paying some regard to Miss Jane Dawson, whose patient affection surely was deserving of some reward, no matter how slight.

As for Susan and her concern for their family's pride, the squire understood his daughter very well. Indeed she was like him in so many ways that he had often thought it was a pity that she had been born a girl. It concerned the squire to see his daughter so disturbed by the turn of events precipitated by the arrival of the Woodstones in their midst, and he had listened to her account of the Misses Reardon's card party with some degree of sympathy. Neither could he blame her for her unwillingness to be the object of Sir Rupert Knightly's attention, if her description of that gentleman's general character were accurate.

However, he had been content to say nothing, until this morning when Susan and he found themselves alone at the breakfast table. It was a cloudless day and the windows were open to the soft breeze which brought with it the sweet scent of wallflowers and roses. Having helped himself to a generous portion of his own home-cured ham and allowed Sally to pour him a second glass of ale, the squire settled himself in his high backed chair and gazed thoughtfully at his daughter.

It was clear that Susan had spent a restless night for, although her eyes sparkled with their usual excess of spirit, there were dark smudges under them, and he thought her rather paler than usual as she sat sipping a cup of tea and crumbling her toast. What was clearly needed, the squire thought, was some distraction from her own troubles.

"I did not mention it last night, my dear," he said, "but while you and your mother were gone I had an unexpected visitor."

"Not Sir Rupert, I hope, sir!" Susan replied with an air of trepidation.

The squire leaned back his grizzled head and laughed heartily.

"No, it was not the unfortunate Sir Rupert," he assured her, "but someone close to him. Lord Woodstone put in an appearance soon after you had left. I do not know why it could not have waited until today, but he seemed quite eager to discuss a matter of business with me."

"The north meadow!" Susan declared with a sort of grim satisfaction. "I knew he would not be long in seeking his reward for good behavior at the dance, although after what I said to him, I declare I do not know how he had the audacity . . ."

"Now, wait a minute, my lass," her father interrupted her. "Sometimes I think you are like a young filly which has never known a rein. The

71

fact is, it was the north meadow he had on his mind. But he came to tell me that he had decided not to press for the rental of it. He intends, I think, to lease the Garrow property to the south of the Muir estate if that can be arranged."

"Does he indeed!" Susan exclaimed, making no secret of her surprise.

"Even when I told him that I was inclined to let him have the meadow at the price he mentioned, the gentleman was obdurant," the squire continued, watching his daughter carefully.

"I expect it gave him a deal of satisfaction to prove me wrong," Susan murmured, flushing.

"And I have never seen you so eager to think ill of any family as you are of the Woodstones," her father replied. "It may not suit you to hear me say that I found the gentleman to be far more knowledgeable than I had thought concerning the management of a large estate. Granted he has some newfangled notions which I would be pleased to see better tested before I put them to use, but still I hope to see him succeed; for if he does, I understand he will consider purchasing the Muir estate outright, and, as you know, I have thought for years that it was a pity to see such fine land go to waste."

Having made what was, for him, a very long speech indeed, the squire finished his ale and waited for some response which Susan was not long in providing.

"Whether Lord Woodstone makes a success of being a gentleman farmer or not, Papa," she said

72

firmly, "is quite beside the point. I will not see the people in Thrumhill condescended to. Particularly as they seem to be quite content to let it happen. Lord Woodstone may stay here if he likes. I declare it makes little difference to me. But his mother and her fine friends will delight in making an absurd display of us as yokels, and that I cannot endure. Why, only yesterday, Lady Woodstone rode through the village in her carriage with people pulling their forelocks and making curtsies right and left, while all the time she kept her nose in the air and Lady Knightly, too, not to mention Drusella laughing and pointing as though she were visiting a circus."

"You cannot blame Lord Woodstone for that, my dear," her father said in an amused voice. "Let his mother and her friends play any role they like. It does no harm to you or me, I think."

"It hurts my pride!" Susan exclaimed. "Although if that were all of it, no doubt it could be endured. But there is the matter of Franklin to be considered. Maria Woodstone will find any manner of ways to lead him on until she tires of him, I assure you."

And indeed Susan came closer to the point than she imagined, for at the same moment at Muir Hall, a scheme was being put in motion which was intended to provide Maria with better opportunity for her flirtation than had, as yet, been provided.

"But, Mama," the young lady in question was saying in cajoling tones as she sat with her mother and their guests in the breakfast room, the fine diamond-paned windows of which opened onto a lovely terraced vista. "You cannot say no, because it is too late. Indeed it is!"

"It can never be too late to call off an expedition of the sort you have proposed," Lady Woodstone said in a thin voice.

"I quite agree," said Lady Knightly, twitching her thin nose. "I only hope, Rupert, you have been no party to this plan."

"He wrote the letter, Mama!" Drusella giggled. "Only think, he wrote the letter!"

"It was a note, not a letter," her brother said coolly. "What a gudgeon you are, Drusella! It was sent by hand to the village not half an hour ago. Maria and I expect a reply any moment."

"Do you mean to say, sir, that you lowered yourself sufficiently to address that frightful girl?" his mother exclaimed.

"Only indirectly, ma'am," Sir Rupert replied, exchanging an amused glance with Maria who appeared more pert than usual in a white morning gown which flattered her to the utmost.

"I am not prepared to play guessing games," his mother replied tartly. "Say what you mean and be done with it."

"The note was sent to Mr. Franklin Eaton," Maria replied. "And since I am sure that he will find nothing more delightful than to visit the caves with us, I have ordered a little picnic. Everything is arranged, you see, for the groom has orders to have Rupert's phaeton and our own waiting at the front in half an hour."

"But surely you do not plan to go without a chaperon!" Lady Woodstone exclaimed. "Indeed, I cannot agree that you should go at all."

"Drusella and Rupert must be amused, Mama," Maria said with the assurance of one who knows that she will have her own way.

"Surely they need not be entertained by the Eatons!" Lady Woodstone replied.

"I, for one, would be most pleased if Miss Eaton and her brother will agree to accompany us," Sir Rupert said blandly. "Come, Mama, you need not look at me in quite that peculiar way, surely."

"Your brother will put an end to the idea, Miss," Lady Woodstone said, although she seemed unable to meet her daughter's dancing eyes.

"On the contrary, Mama, when I told him that we were quite determined to go, he only sighed and said that he supposed he must go with us. Indeed, it is quite settled. Rupert will drive one carriage and Mr. Eaton the other, and James will ride mount beside us so that he will not be too crowded."

"I cannot understand James' attitude," Lady Woodstone fretted.

"Why, as soon as he understood that I would not be put off, or Rupert either, he had no choice," Maria replied pertly. "And now I must be off to change."

Thus she cleverly put the interview at an end and in a moment the two elder ladies found themselves alone.

"I cannot think there is too much harm in it, Althea," Lady Woodstone said sensing danger in the manner in which her friend cast her nose about like a hunter scenting a rabbit. "As you well know, I had hoped that Maria would seem more interested than she appears to be in Rupert. But then it will all come right in the end if I give her her head in small matters. Why, she need only spend a few hours in the company of your son and that absurd young Eaton before she will see there is no comparison between the two of them."

"Any girl of *sense* would be sure to make the contrast," Lady Knightly agreed with a dangerous edge to her voice.

"Why, as to that, she might have paid him more heed long before now if Rupert were to show the slightest interest," Lady Woodstone said in an irritated manner.

"It appears he finds more to interest him in Miss Eaton," Lady Knightly said caustically. "Not that I do not understand very well why the gel has put herself out to please him."

"I did not notice that she made any singular effort in that regard during her visit here," Lady Woodstone retorted. "Indeed, I did not hear her address more than two words to him at a time. And the other evening at that regrettable entertainment, she seemed none too eager to take the floor with him."

"That is because she plays her cards cleverly," Lady Knightly retorted. "She knows, no doubt, that a sophisticated young man like Rupert does not stand about waiting for ripe fruit to fall into his hands. Which is more than your daughter seems to comprehend, I might add."

And so while the two ladies set about quarreling, Susan's tête-à-tête with her father was interrupted by Franklin who joined them with his face nearly the same flaming red as his hair. Still it was in his usual laconic manner that he informed his sister that they were to join the Woodstones and their guests on an expedition within the hour.

"Indeed, I will do no such thing!" Susan called after him as he beat a retreat.

And yet she knew she would, as her rueful glance at her father made clear.

"There is no other way I can keep him from making a proposal," she explained impatiently as the squire smiled. "Pray do not think I am anything but out of patience with him. But if no one else will see to his safety, than I am sure I must."

CHAPTER
Eight

*S*ince Squire Eaton's square brick house was on the outskirts of the village, it was only reasonable that the inhabitants of Thrumhill should have been treated to the merry sight of two glossy black phaetons drawn by fine bays rattling past the old inn with its swinging signboard bearing the painted impression of a rather weary looking lion, taking the right turn past the gray stone church and bearing full ahead toward the high road to Wells, while a single horseman mounted on a fine black stallion followed at what might have been considered by some a reluctant pace.

Having been thwarted in her effort to share the same carriage with her brother and Maria Woodstone, Susan found herself seated beside Sir Rupert with only the satisfaction of knowing that

Drusella was placed securely between Franklin and Maria in the forward phaeton. Little of an intimate nature could pass between the two, she knew, with Drusella giggling and twitching beside them and she was left with nothing more to deal with than her companion's inane comments on the weather and the scenery. As for Lord Woodstone, he had contented himself with only the slightest inclination of his head when she had emerged from the house, and there had been something about the hooded look in his dark eyes that told her that not only had this expedition not been his idea but that he had not forgotten the words that had passed between them on the occasion of their last meeting. No doubt, she told herself, he was as reluctant a member of this company as she, having been forced into attendance for the same reason.

Once on the high road, their passage became less bumpy, making a sustained conversation possible and Susan, already having tired of making affirmative responses to such observations as "Dashed fine elms there," and "Top of the trace morning, eh?" decided that since it was apparent that she and Sir Rupert were not to ride in silence, she might as well discover what she could of the attitude Lady Woodstone had taken to this little outing.

"Well now, she would act like a cat on a hot bakestone when she first heard of it," Sir Rupert said with obvious amusement when Susan broached the question to him directly. "Blamed if I didn't think she was going to fly up into the boughs and my mother with her."

"That was because my brother and I were invited, I dare say," Susan ventured.

"Stubble it, I'll choose my own company!" Sir Rupert declared, having the good grace to flush. "Which is as much as Maria and I told her."

"But surely if Lady Woodstone protested . . ."

"Maria can twist Her Ladyship around her little finger," Sir Rupert announced, flicking his whip in an expert manner. "And her brother, too, in most things, though the both of them read her a scold now and then."

"It was more than a 'scold,' I think, when Lord Woodstone brought her down here to the country," Susan said in a low voice, glancing over her shoulder to observe how close the gentleman in question was riding to their carriage.

"Dashed if I didn't think that was a hurly-burly thing to do when I first heard of it, 'pon my word I did," Sir Rupert told her. "Should have known a gel like that would find a way to entertain herself wherever she is. Wish my sister would take a page from her book, 'deed I do."

"And so that is what Miss Woodstone is doing," Susan said carefully, not wishing to be drawn into a discussion of Drusella's doubtful social prospects. "Entertaining herself, that is?"

"By gad it would beat the Dutch if she ever did anything else!" Sir Rupert exclaimed. "Not that I'd be such a muckworm as to let her set her cap for me."

And with that he sat up very straight indeed, no doubt fancying himself a very fine figure indeed, with his beaver hat tilted well to the side and his cravat billowing in the wind.

"And has she?" Susan said idly. "Set her cap for you, I mean?"

"No doubt she will when it takes her fancy," Sir Rupert declared bravely. "Not but what she could spare the pains with a fellow like myself who knows his own mind."

And with that he gave Susan such a glance as to make her change the subject at once. Indeed, for the next few miles she rattled on at a great rate about the beauty of the landscape, all of which took very little effort on her part since it consisted of gently rounded hills squared by low stone walls and hedgerows into a soft patchwork of golden mustard and apple-green wheat. But all the time her mind fretted the question of what Maria would be up to next, and it was with a sense of relief that she saw them approach the gorge within which the caves were located.

At the entrance to the narrow ravine the phaetons were brought to a halt and a decision was reached that they should picnic first and explore after. Then it was that the gentlemen made themselves handy with the heavy-ladened baskets and the rugs which had been brought to protect the ladies from the damp, and soon they were seated to a far from light collation consisting of cold chicken and ham, sweetmeats of all varieties, various creams and jellies, not to mention an extraordinary display of sweets and such fruits as the season provided. For the ladies there was ratafia, and for the gentlemen slim bottles of claret.

To her surprise, Susan found her appetite had not deserted her, thanks, perhaps, as much to the fresh air as to the fact that Lord Woodstone had stationed himself beside her brother and had engaged him in a conversation concerning a new sort of telescope he had seen displayed in London. Having thus been forced to put a pause to her flirtation, Maria pouted to no avail while Drusella set to like a trencherman, and even Sir Rupert allowed himself to be distracted by the variety of food and drink at his command.

Franklin was the first to discover that Maria had wandered off, and from his exclamations of concern it was apparent that he thought it probable that she was impatient with him for not having been at attention accompanying her. Before anyone could stop him, he was hurrying along the narrow path which led into the gorge and could soon be heard calling her name.

"I should have known the jade would think of some way to get him alone," Susan heard Lord Woodstone mutter as he started to his feet. "Come, Miss Eaton. No doubt you know the area better than any of us. Where will she have gone, do you think?"

Since these were the first words he had addressed to her since that evening at the assembly, Susan was not surprised to hear the roughness of his tone. Still, she flushed with annoyance.

"I should have thought you would have thought first of the danger, sir," she said reprovingly. "At least I am certain that was what was in my brother's mind."

"Are there many caves then, and are they deep?" Lord Woodstone demanded. "I would have put my foot down at the start if I had thought she would have played this sort of trick."

"We would be better off to go and find her, I think," Susan retorted. "Franklin knows the place as well as I do, for we have been brought here now and then since we were children, but he will need our help if she is any distance ahead of us for there are any number of openings into which she might stray."

"She will not let herself remain long out of his sight, I warrant," Lord Woodstone said grimly.

"If that's the case, why not leave them alone, eh?" Sir Rupert declared, his voice slightly slurred as is often the case with one who has imbibed too deeply. "Better yet, Woodstone, take my sister for company, and Miss Eaton and I will hold the fort here."

But Susan was already hurrying along the path. "You're in no state to come with us, Knightly," she heard Lord Woodstone mutter. And this suggestion being followed by the sound of breaking glass, Susan deduced without turning that Sir Rupert had found that true enough when he had tried to rise.

Although the gorge was familiar enough to Susan, she did not find it an inviting place, for the rocks on either side successfully shut out the sun, and the caves, most of them too small to enter, seemed to stare at her with blank eyes. To her dismay she found that Franklin was already no longer in sight.

"I wonder you allowed this expedition, sir," she said in a low voice as Lord Woodstone took her arm to help her over a particularly rough spot. "Indeed, I thought from what you said once that you were willing to take pains to prevent just this sort of eventuality."

"I am not my sister's jailer, Miss Eaton," he said stiffly, "whatever you may think. It was one thing to bring her down from London, and quite another to prevent her from going on a simple outing with anyone she cared to invite. Particularly since Sir Rupert seemed so keen on making you and your brother part of the group."

"And do you think I encouraged him to do so, sir?" Susan demanded. "For if you do . . ."

She broke off since, at that moment coming to the mouth of one of the larger caves, she caught a glimpse of her brother just inside the entrance.

"Franklin!" she exclaimed. "Have you found her?"

But before he could answer her, Maria's voice could be heard echoing from somewhere deep inside.

"Oh, dear!" Maria cried. "I think that I have lost my way! Are you there, dear Mr. Eaton? I will stand quite still and call out now and then until you have found me."

Muttering something about the necessity of going after her at once, Franklin started into the cave, but Susan caught him by the coattails.

"You will do nothing of the sort, Frank!" she exclaimed in a low voice. "We have no light and . . ."

"There are candles back in the carriage," Lord Woodstone muttered. "Perhaps you will do me the favor of fetching them, Mr. Eaton, and then I will see to my sister."

"Think before you act, sir!" Susan told him. "You have told me that your sister is headstrong. If you go after her, calling and holding a candle, what will be her response, do you think?"

"No doubt she will be angry to have had me interfere," Lord Woodstone told her.

"And if she is angry, is she apt to do anything foolish?" Susan replied, still holding Franklin firmly. "Seek to avoid you, perhaps? I do not think she is as yet far enough into the cave to allow her a choice of passages. But if she decides to lead you a chase the results may be unfortunate, indeed."

"Then what do you suggest, pray?" Lord Woodstone demanded. "She may do the same if your brother goes to fetch her, for quite another purpose."

"What I propose is this," Susan said quietly. "Had you had opportunity to make her a response before we arrived, Frank?"

Her brother, evidently in a state of some confusion, shook his head.

"Then she will be content to stay where she is and call until you make some answer," Susan told him. "And that you will not do."

"Shall we simply leave her there, do you mean?" Lord Woodstone said with heavy sarcasm.

"From where she stands, doubtless she can see the light from the cave's entrance," Susan said evenly. "If you will both stand aside, I will bring her out quickly enough."

"You do not mean that you will attempt to go after her without any illumination!" Lord Woodstone exclaimed. "Indeed, I will not allow it!"

"I will not take a step from where I stand, sir," Susan told him. "Permit me to presume that I know something of what transpires in a lady's mind."

"Which I'll be damned is more than I do!" Lord Woodstone declared. But all the same, he stood aside, taking Franklin with him.

"Dear Mr. Eaton!" Maria cried before more than a few seconds had elapsed. "Do come and find me before I lose my way!"

"I am here, Miss Woodstone!" Susan called, cupping her mouth with her hand. "It does no good to call for my brother since he and the others have gone ahead to look elsewhere. Now come. You can see the light, I think. Simply walk toward it. I will wait for you."

A long silence followed. Behind her Susan

heard someone chuckle and knew that it was not her brother.

The sound of a scuffed rock sounded from inside the cave.

"Are you coming, Miss Woodstone?" Susan cried. "Of course if you prefer to remain inside you must not let me hurry you. Of course, there are pits everywhere. Straight drops into wells of water. And then, of course, there are the rats."

A scream was heard and then another, each much closer to the entrance than the one preceding it.

"Now if you do not wish to have me found out in Banbury tale, gentlemen," Susan said, turning to glance over her shoulder, "you will take a stroll along the path so that you will not be in sight when she emerges. We have played a trick for her own good, I'm sure, but I think it just as well she should not be aware of it."

And so it was that Maria Woodstone emerged from the cave to find Susan Eaton waiting for her alone, as she had said.

"It was a foolish thing to do," Susan told her. "But we will say nothing of it to the others, if you like."

"Oh, dear Miss Eaton, are there really rats inside there?" Miss Woodstone cried.

Putting her arm about the other's waist, Susan assured her that snakes were not the least of the small nuisances which might have slid across her feet. And thus it was that when Lord Woodstone and young Mr. Eaton made their return down the path they found Maria with her arms clasped about Susan's neck in an access of gratitude. And although Susan was not to notice it, there was gratitude and not a little admiration in the eyes of Lord Woodstone as he and her brother followed the two young ladies back to the picnic ground.

CHAPTER
Nine

It was tea time when the two smart phaetons swung up the drive to Squire Eaton's house and the long, thick rays of afternoon sunlight glistening on the casement windows of the front sitting room illuminated the curious faces of the two Misses Jackson as Franklin stepped down from the first carriage and surrendered the reins to Lord Woodstone who had already tied his horse to the back of the conveyance. As for Susan, she had first to submit to the last of the many embraces which Maria Woodstone had showered on her since her rescue before she could alight. Then the company from Muir Hall was off and Susan was being greeted by not only Ruth and Priscilla Jackson but Jane Dawson as well.

"Fancy!" Ruth exclaimed as Franklin bowed

and made his way past the cluster of young ladies with a distant look in his eyes. "I declare you forgot that you had asked us tea, Susan. But, never mind. Your mother has entertained us well enough."

"And we quite understand, my dear," her sister added, presenting a rather withered cheek to be kissed. "No doubt you were so excited by the proposal of a picnic that everything else was driven from your mind."

"It was not excitement that did it, I think," Jane said dryly, watching Franklin climb the stairs. "All is well, I take it?"

"But come and join us in another cup of tea," Priscilla cried as Susan exchanged a conspiratorial nod with her friend. "Betty has called your mother off to deal with some disaster in the kitchen and so you must make up for your absence by telling us all the news."

"First we must tell her ours!" Ruth declared, leading the way into the sitting room. "Come, Susan. Take off your bonnet and play the hostess at last."

As they took their places about the tea table, Susan was relieved to find that she was not to be pressed about the events of her day abroad since Ruth and Priscilla, at least, were full of their own excitement.

"Such a colorful parade as I never saw before!" Ruth Jackson cried.

"Such handsome uniforms!" Priscilla declared with enthusiasm.

"So many officers!"

"La, it quite took my breath away!"

"The garrison has arrived," Jane Dawson said in a low voice.

"To think that they will be stationed not a mile out of the village!" Ruth exclaimed in delight.

"And Patience told us . . ."

"You know how quickly she hears all the news!"

". . . that the officers are expecting us to provide them with all manner of entertainment."

"Mother is already making plans for another dance at the assembly room!"

"She says that we must call it that now, to lend some *éclair!*"

"And my pink silk is to be turned and cut a bit more to the fashion!"

Susan and Jane exchanged amused glances as they sipped their tea and listened. What a relief it was, Susan thought, to be back among friends again and even though, in the past, the Jackson sisters had tired her with their raptures, she was good natured enough to hope that this time their hopes would not be blighted.

"There is one thing to be glad of, at least," she told Jane when, at last, they were alone together, Ruth and her sister having decided to drop by the Misses Reardon's in the hope of hearing any further news the artful Patience might have gathered.

"And that is that they have been distracted

93

from any excitement which Muir Hall might provide them," Jane said, finishing the sentence for her.

"Precisely so," Susan agreed. "Although after what happened today I think it possible that I will hear more from that quarter than I care to hear."

"Sir Rupert?"

"I sincerely hope not," Susan told her. "No, it is Maria Woodstone I am thinking of."

And then she went on to tell her friend something of what had transpired at the caves.

"It seems that now she considers me her dearest friend," Susan concluded. "Nothing would do but that I sit between her and Franklin on the way home. And she was full of how we should be as close as sisters in the future."

"Is it a ploy do you think?" Jane asked thoughtfully, and Susan knew she was thinking of Franklin.

"Indeed I do not think it is," she told her friend, "for she did not pay him an ounce of attention once I had 'rescued' her. That is how she refers to it, you see."

"You are her new enthusiasm," Jane said in a low voice. "What a strange creature she is, to be sure."

"More artless than I had thought," Susan agreed.

"And how does your brother take this transfer of affection?"

"I do not think he knows what to make of it,"

Susan replied. "As for me, I can only hope that he will take notice of how she flits from one thing to the next and learn a lesson from it."

"But all of this means that she will be much about this house," Jane said with a little sigh.

"I expect I could discourage that," Susan replied. "Certainly I do not intend to go to Muir Hall. And yet she made me feel quite sorry for her in a way. She has no friends here and Drusella Knightly amounts to nothing but an irritation."

"There is the garrison, of course," Jane murmured. "I wonder if she will be able to restrain herself from the possibility of so many flirtations?"

"Oh dear, I had not thought of that!" Susan exclaimed. "What a mix-up *that* would be, I'm sure."

And as the two girls speculated, Lady Woodstone at Muir Hall turned her mind to something of a more concrete nature, Drusella having proved herself incapable of keeping the events of this exciting day to herself.

"I declare I want you to hear the gel's story yourself, Regina!" Lady Knightly announced, appearing in her hostess' dressing room with no more preamble than a tap on the door. "Go ahead, Drusella, do! Tell Lady Woodstone what you have just told me about what happened at the caves."

But although Drusella had found it possible to communicate with her own mama of whom she stood in little awe, she was sent into gales of hysterical laughter by the awful look which Lady Woodstone turned on her.

"Perhaps you should administer your vinaigrette, Althea," Lady Woodstone said coldly. "If she were my own daughter, of course, I think a few smart slaps might be more effective. But you have your own way of raising your children, of course."

The look which accompanied this comment left little doubt as to her opinion of Lady Knightly's qualifications as a parent—which so infuriated her that Drusella did, indeed, find herself the recipient of a blow on her boney back.

"And now, perhaps, we can proceed," Lady Woodstone said, reclining on her chaise lounge and snapping open her fan. "What is it that you have to tell me, Drusella?"

But Drusella was not so easily subdued. Opening her mouth in the manner of a fish raised from the water, she managed the word 'cave' and then relapsed into a nervous titter, at the same time stationing herself as far as possible from her mama.

"And what about the caves, pray?" Lady Woodstone demanded.

"Your daughter took the liberty of going into one of them alone, madam," Lady Knightly said, pointing her long nose to the ceiling.

"Did she, indeed?" Lady Woodstone replied. "And yet she arrived home safe and sound, I believe, although I did notice that her gown was somewhat dirtied. If what Drusella has told you is true, of course, she acted foolishly. James should not have allowed it, and I will speak to him accordingly. But I scarcely see why I should have been disturbed in my rest before dinner."

"You put too good a color on your children's affairs, Regina!" Lady Knightly said impatiently. "Drusella tells me that Maria was playing the flirt, as always, and indulged in her little escapade with the distinct expectation that Mr. Eaton would follow her."

Lady Woodstone heaved a great sigh. Granted that it had been her hope in inviting her friend and her offspring to visit Muir Hall that some arrangement might be made at least between Maria and Sir Rupert, she was sensible enough to have seen early on that the two young people were not of a temperament to be attracted to one another. Still, she had dared to hope that there would be safety in numbers. And now it seemed that Maria was as bent on her pursuit of the squire's unfortunate son as she had been when there had been no guests in the house.

"I think your daughter is too fanciful to be believed, my dear Althea," she said in a voice which would have quelled a less determined personage than Lady Knightly. "No doubt she sees romance everywhere which is often the case, I think, when a gel lacks distractions of her own."

"My daughter is no fibster, madam," Lady Knightly said stiffly. "There, I will speak frankly since it is clear that you will not. You know full well that I came here to comfort you in your exile. But I am determined now to return to London tomorrow unless I can be assured that Drusella will not be exposed to any further adventures such as those she has been forced to take part in today."

"I think I know as well as you why you came here," Lady Woodstone replied evenly. "Certain arrangement of affairs is to your advantage as much as it is to mine, I believe. And now, if you will leave me, I will get the truth of the matter from James."

But the truth, when she had it, was as little to Lady Woodstone's liking as her friend's insinuations had been.

"If it had not been for Miss Eaton's common sense, there might well have been a tragedy," he told her as they sat alone in her dressing room.

"If it had not been for Miss Eaton and her brother, sir, the occasion for tragedy might never have arisen," his mother said shrilly. "Certainly this—this incident must have made it quite clear to you that the connection must be broken off at once."

"As for that," Lord Woodstone replied evenly, "some good may have come of today's events, for I believe Maria has transferred her attention from Mr. Eaton to his sister whom she appears to admire excessively."

"And can you tell me, sir, that that is for the good?" Lady Woodstone declared. "Obviously, Miss Eaton would go to any lengths to insure an attachment between this family and hers. No doubt she put Maria up to her—her escapade. I will not have any further correspondence between them, James. Is that understood?"

The matter having thus been brought to a head above stairs, it was continued at dinner when, over the fish course, Lady Knightly announced that it was her intention to return to London tomorrow.

"Then you must be content with the company of my sister and our footman, madam," Sir Rupert declared.

"And what, may I ask you, would keep you here, sir?" his mother demanded, her thin nose twitching impatiently.

"Let us say that I find the rural scene relaxing," Sir Rupert replied, gesturing to the footman to refill his glass.

"That is not a sufficient response to satisfy me, sir," Lady Knightly declared. "May I suggest that you have found yourself entrapped by the charms of a certain Miss Eaton? May I suggest that you are a fool, sir?"

"You may suggest no such thing, madam!" Sir Rupert exclaimed with greater lucidity than was his fashion. "Miss Eaton does not entrap. She is too fine a character for that."

"He speaks the truth, mama," Maria said, raising her glass.

"And you, James? Do you agree?" Lady Woodstone said in a voice which sank like iron to the table.

"You know my opinion better than to ask the

question," Lord Woodstone said in a low voice. And then, as an aside: "No more wine is to be served, Tom."

And Tom complied. But, footman though he was, he did not lack ears to hear. And he had heard enough already to convey certain information to the Misses Reardon's maid with whom he was on very friendly terms, with the result that by the following morning it was common knowledge in the village of Thrumhill that Sir Rupert Knightly was, to all intents and purposes, prepared to offer for Miss Susan Eaton.

CHAPTER
Ten

These were indeed exciting times as the Reardon sisters never tired of saying. Now they not only awoke to the faint sound of reveille and retired to the rolling echo of the sounding of tattoo at ten but there was the added fillip of finding the village streets full of red-coated soldiers, the officers smart with their tricorne felt hats and shining medals. Indeed everyone became quite knowledgeable about the military way of life and there were constant outings to observe maneuvers and target firing and the general orderliness of the camp was much admired by the ladies. Patience became a marching expert and was able to regale her mistresses' company by executing the ordinary, quick and quickest step, holding a broomstick to her shoulder. While Ruth and Priscilla Jackson came to speak of muskets, carbines and pistols with the air of those to whom all manner of weapons of destruction were as familiar as household utensils.

Parson Dawson was discovered to be a student of the Duke of Marlborough's strategy and spoke at length to anyone who would listen about the campaigns of Lille-St. Hubert and Ramillies with as much enthusiasm as though they had happened only yesterday instead of a hundred years before, while Captain Blazemore neglected the brandy bottle to reminisce about his youthful memories of conflict in America where, he declared, the English would never have been beaten had it not been for the perfidy of the French in lending the colonists aid.

As for the Misses Reardon, their prestige in the village had never been higher. If there had been much talk of their father, the general, before, it was nothing to the profusion of fond recollections of the great man's habits, the showing of his portrait which graced the panel over the fireplace, and the delving in boxes and trunks for all manner of memorabilia which ranged from his gold-hilted saber to a few ancient and unused cartridges.

As for the officers, they took such peculiarities in their stride, particularly when, in the case of the Misses Reardon, their patience found its reward in invitations which made it possible for them to continue acquaintances with various young ladies first encountered at the dances held each Thursday night at the assembly room.

Never had Mrs. Jackson been so happily occupied in providing Ruth and Priscilla with opportunities to make a match. Never had Thrumhill's three fiddle players been so constantly occupied. Never had little Miss Jervey, the village seamstress, been so perpetually engaged in the taking out of hems and the putting in of gussets.

It was only to be expected that Maria Woodstone would be caught up in the general excitement, especially as it involved any number of young officers at whom she could bat her eyes with impunity. Her eagerness to be Susan's most intimate friend had, as a consequence, faded since Maria's preoccupations could only be entertained one at a time.

"It took her no time at all to discover that since she was unlikely to meet any of the officers in this house, she would be better off making friends with the Misses Reardon," Susan told Jane with a sigh of relief.

"I wonder that her Mama allows her to spend quite as much time in the village as she does," Ruth replied. "She seems to spend nearly as much time as Ruth and Priscilla parading up and down the street, twirling her parasol and being free enough with her smiles to satisfy every officer in the garrison."

"She pays special attention to Lieuténant Moore," Susan added. "He is the one with the thick blond hair, you know."

"I know," Jane said with a wry smile. "Every young lady in Thrumhill knows Lieutenant Moore. Why, he is as much a flirt as Maria."

"I think that both have met their match," Susan agreed thoughtfully, curling one dark lock around her finger. "But the point is this. At the dances when her brother is in attendance, Miss Woodstone pays very little attention to Lieutenant Moore."

"I had noticed that she was free with her favors," Jane replied. "Poor Franklin . . ."

"Yes, let us return to my brother in a moment," Susan suggested. "I only mean to suggest that Miss Woodstone is exercising a certain measure of deceit. At the assembly hall, for instance, she takes her seat beside me as often as possible, much as though we had become the dear friends she first suggested."

"And why should she do that?" Jane asked.

"I have wracked my mind about it," Susan confessed, "and I can think of nothing else than this. Lord Woodstone is pleased enough to have his sister be my friend, I think, because he fancies that I may teach her common sense and some decorum."

"You think Maria uses you as an excuse to come into the village every day?" Jane said quickly.

"Indeed I am nearly certain of it," Susan told her, "for Lord Woodstone paused beside me just long enough last Thursday night to thank me and I can think of no reason why I deserve his recent gratitude but that."

"And so Maria is coming into Thrumhill every day under false pretenses," Jane said thoughtfully, "and spending her afternoons parading about or attending some soirée or other at the Reardon's."

"And in each instance it seems likely that she will encounter Lieutenant Moore," Susan said in a soft voice. "Of course, Franklin would have it that there is no harm in it as long as he keeps his eye on her."

"What's this you say?" Jane exclaimed, turning pale. "I thought by now he would have seen her for what she is. Why, I saw the pain in his eyes when she danced with everyone else but him last Thursday."

"Rest assured that I did not fail to take the opportunity to talk to him about it," Susan told her. "I thought to find him broken-hearted, but instead he is all obtuseness. He will not see her faults."

"But what excuse can he be making for her behavior?"

"He says," Susan declared, pursing her lips, "that it is only natural that a beautiful young lady who has been forced to leave London with all the opportunities it provides would find her head turned by all the attentions that the garrison officers provide. But, of course, she will settle down as soon as the garrison moves its bivouac to another location, with no harm done.

And then, of course, her attention will be his alone again and the story will end happily for all concerned."

"All of what you have said sounds strangely unlike Franklin," Jane said suspiciously.

"I did not quote him exactly, of course," Susan told her, "for you know how little he has to say about any subject. But, after an hour of interrogating him I came away with the impression that he meant exactly what I have told you. One thing is clear, at least. My brother is firmly convinced that Maria Woodstone's heart is his and his alone."

"I wish that Lieutenant Moore understood that salient point," Jane said dryly.

"And I wish that Lord Woodstone could be made aware that his sister has not cast me in the role of duenna," Susan replied.

The opportunity for her to clarify the matter in question occurred rather more rapidly than she would have had it for, as little as Susan found to fault in Lord Woodstone's behavior, it seemed to her that each time there was an occasion for them to converse, misunderstanding lay in wait for them. And yet the following morning when she looked out her chamber window and saw his dark head bent close to her fathers grizzled one as they talked in the yard, Susan knew that she must not let the chance go a-begging. Quickly donning a primrose and white striped poplin morning gown and pulling her thick curls back and up with an apple-green ribbon, she hurried down the stairs and through the morning coolness of the hall to the front of the house where Lord Woodstone had left his chestnut bay.

It was difficult for Susan to wait patiently although she knew that Lord Woodstone's occasional visits to her father for the purpose of receiving agricultural advice frequently led to prolonged conversations which they both enjoyed. However, it was not long today before the young gentleman in question came striding around the corner of the house, a handsome figure in buff buckskin jacket and trousers, his Wellington boots stained with mud from the courtyard.

"Miss Eaton!" he exclaimed as she stepped forward. "I did not think to see you at as early an hour as this."

"I am accustomed to keep my father's schedule as much as possible," Susan told him. "Or at least to be on hand to breakfast with him when he comes in from the yard. We keep no fancy ways here, sir, as you see."

No sooner had the words left her mouth than she cursed herself for uttering them. What business was it of hers to speak so petulantly as though there were some special point of argument between them?

"I see that you do not," Lord Woodstone said, bowing, but not before Susan thought she saw a trace of wry humor in his eyes.

"I cannot think why I wished to assure you of

it, sir," she went on, aware that the color was rising in her cheeks. "Indeed, I think I am awkward because I find it difficult to ask you the question I must ask."

"And what is that, Miss Eaton?" he said, quite serious now. "But before you tell me, perhaps you will accept my apologies for being so remiss in thanking you in detail, not only for bringing my sister safely from the cave the other day, but for allowing her to be so much in your company. You know my mother well enough to guess how well she likes to see Maria coming to the village, but I think I have persuaded her that, since the models she provided my sister with in London taught her so much foolishness . . ."

"Pray do not continue, sir," Susan said quickly, "for you have answered my question."

"I am sure I do not know how that could be," he said, wrinkling his forehead. "I think I have not told you anything you did not know before. I can only hope Maria has not been too much of a nuisance to you. But she will insist that Knightly drive her down every morning in the gig and since, as he claims, he has little better to do . . ."

"Sir Rupert finds it difficult to believe that others have certain duties they must perform," Susan said quickly for, although she had not mentioned this to Jane, Sir Rupert's arrival in the village every day was nearly as much trouble to her as Maria's. Indeed, she had become accustomed to his appearing at the front door every morning at a bit past eleven, having left Maria in

108

the village. And every day there was some new plan for an excursion which Susan must find an excuse to avoid. Illness had been her latest ploy, she was ashamed to admit even to herself, and although she had never suffered a megrim in her life, she was now, as far as Sir Rupert knew, their constant victim.

"There is no way I can keep him from going where he likes," Lord Woodstone said. "But as for my sister, if you find her too much of a trial, you must tell me."

"Indeed, sir," Susan said evenly, "she is no trial at all since I rarely see her, and then only if I happen to be shopping in the village or drop in to visit the Misses Reardon."

For a moment he looked as though he did not understand her and then his face grew darker and his eyes narrowed as he took a step or two to bring him closer.

"Do you mean to say that my sister has not been at this house for the past week?" he demanded harshly.

"No, she has not, sir!" Susan said sharply. "And there is no use looking as though you blamed me for it since I had no way of knowing that I was supposed to play the role of her nursemaid!"

"She has used you to trick me," Lord Woodstone said in a thick voice.

"She may have used my name but she has made no use of me, sir," Susan assured him, furious at the implication that she had had some hand in Maria's deceit. "Now, as for Sir Rupert, that is another matter. Would you say that he must have realized that your mother and you believed Maria was to spend the day with me when he brought her to the village?"

She had provided him someone to blame and, although his face grew darker, Susan saw that his anger was no longer directed at her.

"Dash it, of course Knightly knew where she was supposed to go!" he exclaimed, striking the fist of one hand against the open palm of the other. "He will hear something more of this, I assure you."

"I hope he may," Susan said, "and your sister, as well. I would have told you betimes, but it did not occur to me until the other day when talking with a friend that your sister might have used me as an excuse to come into the village."

"I suppose the garrison is at the heart of the matter," Lord Woodstone said grimly. "Can you do me the favor of telling me what the chit has been up to, Miss Eaton?"

"I can tell you no more than what I have casually observed," Susan replied, "for I have made no attempt to spy on her."

"No one has made that accusation," he said impatiently.

"I did not say they had, sir. You are too touchy by far, I think, but that is by the by."

"Indeed it is. I only want to know what my sister has been up to. Surely that is understandable enough, unless you support her deceit."

"I think I have made it clear enough that I do not, sir!"

For a moment they both paused, breathless, and stared at one another.

"I do not think you need to worry yourself overmuch," Susan said finally. "Your sister has amused herself in her usual fashion but there has been no harm to it that I can see. When she walks down the village streets, she is in the company of other young ladies who have much the same preoccupations as herself, and certainly she could not be better chaperoned than she is at the Misses Reardon's."

"I cannot put as fine a light on it as you do, I fear," he told her, his dark eyes like gimlets. "What a fool I was to think that by removing her from London I could solve a problem!"

"You must not blame yourself, sir," Susan said in a low voice. "Your sister has a strong will, that is all."

"That is enough, I assure you."

"You have only this to fear, I think," Susan said taking courage from the fact that the young man made no effort to leave her. If he had asked her for advice she might have disclaimed her ability to give it, but under these circumstances she found it irresistible not to speak her mind.

"And what is that?" he asked her when she paused.

"That she should marry unhappily."

"Ah, there is more to it than that, I fear," he told her with heavy irony. "If you do not believe

111

me, our mother can make it clear enough. Maria must not marry beneath her. I do not speak of money. She has her own inheritance. It is in the social sense that I speak."

"I understand you," Susan said dryly. "It would not do, of course, to dilute blue blood with the red."

"That is not *my* notion!" Lord Woodstone exclaimed. "My only fear is that she will find her own head turned, of a sudden, and slip lightly into an alliance which she will soon have cause to regret."

"But if she must marry at her station," Susan said thoughtfully, "and if there seems to be no way you can keep her from playing the flirt, would it not be better if she returned to London? There, at least, there would be gentlemen of the proper rank to suit her. And if she remains here . . ."

"Have you seen her show any special preferences for one of the officers?" he demanded, tense again.

Susan thought of Lieutenant Moore with his boy's face above his white soldier's waistcoat and cravat. But then she recalled that the look in the soldier's blue eyes showed no more or less infatuation than Maria Woodstone must have awakened in the breast of scores of gentlemen, including Franklin. And so she shook her head and thought, as she did so, that she had at least prevented any encounter between the furious man before her and a young fellow who had

112

done no more than many another would have done.

Besides, she told herself, as Lord Woodstone, grim and distracted, took his leave, Maria would make no more appearances in the village, sitting beside Sir Rupert in the gig. She could only hope that Lord Woodstone would find a way to prevent them both from coming.

CHAPTER
Eleven

S*ince it was Maria*
Woodstone's custom to keep to her bed late on
the mornings following a dance, no one at Muir
Hall was surprised when, that next Friday, she
was not down to breakfast. But when luncheon
came and went without her putting in an appearance, her abigail, Sally, was dispatched to
her chamber to rouse her. A few minutes later
the girl appeared in the drawing room in a state
of considerable agitation to inform Lady Woodstone and her guests that Maria's bed had not
been slept in and that a small valise together
with certain dressing articles and a portion of her
wardrobe was missing.

At once Lady Woodstone fell into a shocking
state of hysteria, collapsing on the sofa and
shrieking that her little girl had been kidnapped

until, by dint of applying a vinaigrette directly to her nose, Lady Knightly managed to reduce her to such a state of coughing and sputtering as to make words impossible. Meanwhile Rupert, who had received the news with considerable interest, declared with monotonous repetition that Maria had 'flown the coop' at last, while Drusella lurked in a corner, giggling nervously.

"Now, we must all be as sensible as possible," Lady Knightly declared when a relative degree of order had been restored and Lady Woodstone was sniffling into her handkerchief. "Are you quite certain that Miss Woodstone did not make up the bed herself, Sally?"

"La, ma'am, she would never think of doing anything of the sort," the abigail replied. "Why, I do not think she would have the first notion as to how to go about it!"

"Surely, Mama," Rupert said jovially, "you are not suggesting that Maria arose, made her bed, packed a valise and went out for a little walk about the garden."

"There is no need to be flip, sir!" his mother exclaimed as Lady Woodstone fell to wailing again. "I merely wish to explore all possibilities."

"Kidnapped!" Lady Woodstone gasped.

Rupert observed that it was unlikely that anyone bent on abduction would take the time to allow his victim to pack a few favorite toilet articles and gowns.

"No, you must face the obvious truth," he went on. "The gel has eloped. Just the sort of ro-

116

mantic nonsense which might appeal to her. 'Pon my soul, it don't surprise me, now I come to think of it. Half way to Gretna Green by now, I've no doubt."

If his intention were to comfort Lady Woodstone, he met with little success, since that usually dignified personage, on hearing his opinion, began to fling herself from side to side like a pendulum, while Lady Knightly vainly attempted to apply the vinaigrette once more.

"No doubt it is the squire's son who is responsible," Lady Knightly said grimly. "I told you, Regina, that I thought it was the worst sort of folly to allow Maria to lead him on the way she did."

"Kidnapped!" Lady Woodstone cried, intent on clinging to her original ideas. "James must be sent for at once. Kidnapped!"

"Go and tell one of the footmen to fetch him, Sally," Lady Knightly said grimly. "I believe I heard him say at breakfast that he was off to see someone named Garrow or something of the sort about a west meadow, whatever that may mean."

The abigail taking flight in an instant, Drusella began to titter even louder, causing her mother to threaten dire consequences unless she could control herself at once.

"I think she wants to show you something, Mama," Rupert said blandly. "At least she is waving something which looks very like a letter in your general direction."

"Do not distract me now, Drusella," Lady

117

Knightly muttered. "Cannot you see that Lady Woodstone is on the verge of a complete collapse?"

And, indeed, that seemed very likely to be true, since her friend was now giving every indication of being about to swoon, gasping for air like a fish pulled out of water.

"This will do the trick. Damme if it won't," Rupert declared, pouring a glass full of brandy from the decanter on one of the side tables and administering it to Lady Woodstone with all the delicacy of a horse doctor dosing a sick stallion, the result being that his hostess began to sputter wildly and clutch at her throat.

Drusella took advantage of this distraction to force the letter into her mother's hands and at once, on seeing the hand in which the name of Lord Woodstone was written, Lady Knightly announced that, unless she was mistaken, this was a message form Maria, addressed to her brother.

"But how did you come by this?" she demanded. "Answer me directly, Drusella, or I declare I will not be responsible!"

"Yes, where did you get it?" Lady Woodstone cried with more lucidity than she had displayed until this moment.

"Why, it was underneath my door this morning, Mama," the girl replied, retreating to her corner and making a clear attempt to maintain her composure.

"Why would Maria have left it there if she

meant her brother to have it?" Lady Woodstone demanded. "It makes no sense at all!"

"Why, I think it makes a good bit of sense," Rupert declared. "She knew that Drusella would arise late and that James would have left the house by the time it was found. It gave her more time, you see, in the likely event that she would be followed."

"Maria would never be capable of such deviousness!" Lady Woodstone declared, apparently totally restored by the appearance of a folded and sealed bit of paper. "But that is beside the point! Give it to me, Althea! We must see what it says."

"But it is addressed to your son!" Lady Knightly protested, but all to no avail since her friend proceeded to snatch the letter and tear it open. And then, having scanned the words, she gave a little cry and did well and truly swoon at last.

Meanwhile, the footman, Tom, having been alerted by Sally as to what had happened, was off on his way to fetch his master from the west meadow and it was, no doubt, understandable that he should make a pause in the village to have a word with Patience at the Misses Reardon's kitchen door.

Thus it was that Patience was able to serve up for luncheon an even tastier treat than the elderly sister's guests had anticipated.

"Run off!" the first Miss Reardon cried. "Why, how could the gel do such a thing?"

"And with whom?" her sister demanded.

"To where is even more to the point, I should think," Captain Blazemore declared.

"Lady Woodstone must be quite distraught," Mrs. Lawson observed wisely.

"Young Lord Woodstone will be in the devil of a temper when he hears!" her husband announced. "I shouldn't like to be the fellow she's eloped with, 'pon my soul I would not."

"But who can that be?" Mrs. Jackson cried.

"Could it be Franklin, do you suppose?" her elder daughter, Ruth, demanded.

"La, she has spent enough time ogling him these past weeks!" Priscilla announced. "Oh, dear! Oh, dear! If it is Franklin . . ."

"I do not think it can be, miss," Patience announced, having applied her sharp eyes to the view from one of the front windows, "for he is coming down the street just now together with his sister and your daughter, Mr. Dawson."

"Well, I am glad of that, at least," the parson said in a relieved voice. "Franklin is too fine a chap to be mixed up in an elopement. Indeed, I do not know what the world is coming to."

Declaring in unison that Susan and Jane must hear the news, the Jackson sisters rushed out of the house, forgetting their bonnets in their excitement, and, within as few minutes as was physically possible, had conveyed their gossip to the two friends.

For a moment Jane and Susan simply looked at one another. Neither, Susan thought, had

120

guessed that Maria's flirtations would lead to something like this. She was roused from her reflections when she heard Priscilla Jackson call out her brother's name. Turning, she saw Franklin weaving an uncertain way down the street in the direction of their house.

"We never should have broken it to him so abruptly!" Ruth Jackson declared. "Only see the way he walks, like someone in his cups!"

"But, of course, his heart must be quite broken!" her sister replied in the excited manner of one who hopes to see a melodrama enacted before her eyes.

Susan felt the pressure of Jane Dawson's hand on her arm and responded accordingly.

"We must go after him," she said.

"Oh, but he will not want to see me at a time like this," her friend demured.

"But surely, you must want to hear Patience tell the story herself!" Ruth Jackson exclaimed. "I intend to have her make another recital at once. Who knows what details she may have forgotten in the first announcement!"

"I think we must save that particular treat for another time," Susan said dryly. "Come along, Jane. You must lend me your support."

As they followed in Franklin's path, past the church and the inn and the greengrocer's shop, the sight of a passing officer from the garrison in his red jacket made her catch her breath.

"Oh dear," she murmured. "It did not occur to

121

me until this second that I am in part responsible for what has happened."

"How could that be?" Jane Dawson demanded. "There was no way you could have prevented Miss Woodstone from doing as she liked. Why, even her own family . . ."

"Lord Woodstone could have taken steps to stop her if he had only known that she was keeping company with Lieutenant Moore," Susan said in a low voice.

And, with that, she explained how it was that Lord Woodstone had discovered from her the other day that his sister was not spending her days in the village at the squire's house.

"But, as I thought it was only a passing fancy on Maria's part, I said nothing about her tête-à-têtes with the lieutenant. Indeed, I only mentioned that she was often at the Misses Reardon's which must have sounded innocent enough to him. If only I had been completely open with him there might have been no elopement."

"You must not blame yourself," Jane Dawson said firmly. "No doubt I would have made the same decision had I been you. The girl was such a butterfly that no one could have predicted this."

"But he even asked me if she had shown a preference for any of the officers," Susan said, not bothering to hide her dismay. "Now, of course, I must tell him everything and he will have every right to be angry."

"Does it matter much to you if he is?" Jane Dawson asked her, pulling her friend out of the way of a passing wagon.

Finding her friend's eyes too penetrating, Susan did not meet them for long. "Well, of course it is of no particular consequence," she said, tossing her head. "Do not think I mean to hesitate. I will send him a note mentioning my oversight. It will be some help to him, I think, if he goes in search of his sister, as I am certain that he will."

"I expect that would the only proper thing to do," Jane Dawson replied. "Here, we have reached your gate. Truly, I do not think that I will come inside with you. Franklin is bound to be distraught and will want no audience in attendance."

"*You* do not constitute an audience," Susan declared, taking her friend's arm more firmly. "Indeed, seeing you may remind him that certain members of our sex may be trusted."

But, despite Susan's best intentions, her brother would not listen to consolation. Indeed, they entered the house to find Mrs. Eaton peering up the stairwell with a bemused expression in her eyes.

"Whatever is the matter with your brother, my dear?" she said to Susan. "Why, if I did not know better, I would think he was quite tipsy, for he blundered past me as though he were walking in the dark, and now, I think, he has locked himself inside his room."

It did not take Susan long to ascertain that that was precisely what the young man had done. And, although she hammered at his door for quite five minutes or longer, he would make no response.

"Oh dear, do you think he will do himself an injury?" her mother cried when Susan rejoined her and her friend at the foot of the stairs. "Jane has just been telling me what has happened. Poor, poor infatuated boy!"

"He does indeed behave more like a boy than a man," Susan replied. "But there it is. There is no help for it. Perhaps Papa will be able to reason with him when he comes home. And, in the meantime, I have a letter to write and send to Muir Hall. Come, Jane, and help me compose it for, I declare, it will be no very pleasant task."

CHAPTER
Twelve

However, as events would have it, Lord Woodstone was destined not to receive Susan's carefully composed letter until the early hours of the next morning when he returned from a search which had taken him many miles abroad from Thrumhill. His first response, when hearing the news of his sister's elopement from Tom, was to leap on his horse and go after her. Reason told him that if it were a true elopement, the couple would be headed north toward Scotland where licenses were not required, but he had not gone many miles along the high road, stopping to enquire, first at this inn and then another, before realizing that the fact that he could give no description of the man Maria was with would prove a great hindrance. Still, fury and anxiety drove him on until nightfall when he was forced to admit to himself that either the couple had not traveled in this direction at all, or that the man had been clever enough to see to it that Maria was kept hidden.

Brooding over a glass of mulled wine in front of a blazing fire in the public room of the last inn at which he stopped, Lord Woodstone faced the fact that, for the present, at least, he was defeated. Doubtless he had been a fool to have left Thrumhill without first making an attempt to give a name and face to his sister's companion. An hour later, having strengthened himself with a meal of sorts, he was on his way back to Muir Hall which he reached the next morning, begrimed and exhausted, to find Susan's letter waiting for him.

Lord Woodstone's first response was relief that someone had a clue to the identity of the man his sister had eloped with. But, after he had bathed and made a change of clothing, he was aware of a growing anger that he had not been told of Lieutenant Moore's existence earlier. 'No doubt I was mistaken in not mentioning him to you when you asked me so expressly . . .' one of her sentences began. Well, it was far more than a mistake, and that was what he would tell her directly. Rage mingled with disappointment when he considered how much he had counted on her common sense, at least.

As he descended the broad central staircase of the manor house, Lord Woodstone reflected that it was fortunate, at least, that it was still too early for his mother or her guests to be about. But, on his way past the breakfast room, he discovered that Rupert had not lain abed, as was his habit. Taking him by the arm, the young man gave him some account of what had happened in his absence.

"Damme, I had to bear the brunt of it!" he exclaimed gruffly. "Your mother passed from swoons to hysterics like someone quite demented, until I had the sense to call the doctor who put an end to it with a stiff dose of laudanum. Drusella takes the whole thing as a great joke, of course, which is an annoyance in itself, and Mama would not let me leave the house, although I wanted to go into the village to make enquiries."

"Which is precisely what I intend to be about now," Lord Woodstone said abruptly. "You can let them know that my first search met with no success but that I mean to pursue it when I have some further information at hand."

"In my opinion, you ought to wash your hands of it," Sir Rupert declared. "Once the filly's reached Gretna Green, there's the end of it. 'Pon my soul, that's the best you can hope for. Just as likely the fellow had no intention of marriage from the start and she'll be back in a fortnight with her tail between her legs."

Biting back an angry response, Lord Woodstone left the house and had a fresh horse saddled. It was not quite nine when he lowered the brass knocker on the squire's front door.

Betty being busy in the kitchen and her mother on some business upstairs, it fell to Susan to answer the summons, although who could be calling so early she could not guess. On seeing Lord Woodstone, she gave a little gasp.

"I came to thank you for your letter, Miss Eaton," he said stiffly. "And to assure you that I wish the information could have been given to me earlier in order that this disaster might have been avoided. But there is no use in recriminations. What I want now is your assistance."

"You shall have it, sir," Susan assured him, sensing that this was no time to make further apologies. That he was furious both with her and with his sister she was certain. But there was no help for that now.

"Will you step inside, sir?" she said in a low voice. "We can talk in the parlor."

"I would prefer the garden," Lord Woodstone replied in a flat voice. "We are less likely to be disturbed there, I think."

With a nod, Susan led the way down a gravel path to where a trellis covered with pink roses sheltered a bench. She took a seat there, making a business of smoothing the skirts of her blue muslin gown to hide a sudden awkwardness, for she sensed how great an effort he was making to hide his anger with her.

"Very well," Lord Woodstone said, clasping his hands behind him as he paced back and forth before her, the sun glittering on the high polish of his Wellington boots. "I will tell you first that

I have been on the road for all but a few hours since my footman brought me the news yesterday, and I could find no trace of my sister anywhere. No innkeeper had caught a sight of her. I even asked the farmers in the fields, but to no avail. Now I realize that I must know more of this fellow Moore than simply his name. I must have a description. And I must know something of his background. Where he came from. And his character. Whether or not he can be counted on to behave honorably. I will go to the garrison commander, of course, in due time. But first I intend that you should tell me everything you know that might pertain."

He could not keep the harshness from his voice, and even though Susan told herself that he must be exhausted and that, indeed, there were dark shadows under his eyes to prove it, she felt distressed in a way which was new to her.

"I cannot tell you much, I fear," she said. "Except that Lieutenant Moore is very young—not over twenty I would think—and that he is fair. He stands about your height, I think. Ah, and there is this! You have seen him yourself several times at the dances on Thursday nights. Perhaps you remember the officer your sister took the floor with first last Thursday."

"They all look very much alike to me," he muttered. "Each time I looked, Maria seemed to have a different companion, but I cannot remember their faces."

A thought struck him. "How is it," he went

on, "that if she were so seriously involved with someone as to have warranted elopement not four days later, she did not give him more exclusive attention?"

"No doubt, if their plans were already made, she was careful not to do so," Susan suggested cautiously.

"Maria was never cautious enough to be sly," Lord Woodstone observed.

"But it may be that finding herself in love for the first time . . ."

"In love!" He seemed to fling the words at her. "My sister is too giddy for such a thing. Her fancy leads her this way and that with no direction. No doubt his proposal intrigued her. It was another game she could play. Certainly, I doubt that she thought seriously of the consequences."

"We can only hope that is not the case," Susan murmured. "If it is a love match, all may be well in the end."

"Romantic nonsense!" he exclaimed. "You know my sister better than that, I think."

Susan found her own temper rising. "Granted that Miss Woodstone has not given evidence of forming serious attachments in the past," she declared, "you must remember that she is as human as the rest of us, and, as a consequence, genuine affection is not beyond the realm of possibility."

For a moment she thought that he was about to lash out at her but then it became clear that he was determined to remain in control of his self-possession. His dark eyes became almost oblique.

"Whether or not my sister is capable of 'genuine affection,' as you put it," he said sardonically, "is beside the point. The fact is that she is not of age and that one thing, at least, is clear. The lieutenant has taken advantage of a situation in a way which casts considerable doubt on his character. I think you will not argue with me about that, at least."

"I am no more interested in arguments than you are, sir," Susan said stiffly. "As to his character, I know little of it. I never saw him act other than as an officer and a gentleman."

"Until now," Lord Woodstone reminded her.

"Very well. Until now. But from what I saw of him, I thought him to be a—how shall I put it?—a light-hearted fellow, but sincere. There was nothing about him of the roué. I do not think he is the sort to lead a young woman astray and then have done with her which, in this case, would be the worst thing."

"Your knowledge of the sort of man you make reference to comes from novels, I assume," Lord Woodstone said dryly. "On that account, I will take it as seriously as it deserves. You will admit, I expect, that this fresh-faced chap might be well interested in my sister's fortune."

The slur did not go unnoticed. Susan flushed.

"That is quite possible," she said stiffly. "But I must add that you seem determined to prove me a romantic fool which, I assure you, I am not. I only hoped to remind you that this may not be the complete disaster you think it. I thought to hold out some hope, but I see that I was wrong in doing so."

"If that was your intention, you must be commended," Lord Woodstone told her. "You are very fond of commendation, I think."

"You are unfair!" Susan declared, rising. "I have already admitted in my letter to an error. I should have told you when you asked me that I had seen your sister several times in Lieutenant Moore's company. I thought it a simple flirtation and I was mistaken. But I have done everything I could to make amends."

Lord Woodstone began to speak, but she would not give him the opportunity.

"Let me remind you, sir, that we cannot be certain that it was Lieutenant Moore your sister eloped with. It seems the most certain possibility, but, were I you, I would go to the garrison commander at once and discover if he is missing. Has he taken a proper leave or is he gone without permission? Has he been guilty of similar indiscretions in the past? You speak of novels and romantic fancies! On the contrary, I would have you take practical steps, and those as soon as possible."

She flung herself a few steps up the path toward the house and then turned to look back at him. He was staring after her with an expression in his hooded eyes that she could not decipher. No doubt, she thought, he was thinking

132

of a final insult. But she would let him punish her no further.

"One other thing," she said. "I think I told you that during those afternoons your sister was supposed to be with me, she was at the Misses Reardon's house facing the green. It may well be that she often met Lieutenant Moore there. In that case, those two ladies may know something of whatever plans she made with him, although if they did I am surprised that the entire village does not know of it by now. But if you make enquiries there, I suggest that a milder tone be used than that with which you have addressed me!"

And, with that parting remark, she left him, slamming the door of the house behind her. Her mother was waiting in the corridor, and from the expression on her face Susan knew that her encounter with Lord Woodstone had not gone unobserved.

"Is his sister found?" Mrs. Eaton demanded.

"No, she is not!" Susan exclaimed, running up the stairs.

"You must tell Franklin, my dear!" her mother called after her.

"I will tell him nothing until he decides to come out of his room, Mama," Susan cried, trying to keep her voice from choking.

And, indeed, as she closed the door of her own chamber behind her, Franklin's folly was the furthest thing from her mind.

CHAPTER
Thirteen

Susan did not find life particularly pleasant during the next few days. In the first place, perverse nature which could, at least, have made some attempt to provide the comfort of mellow sunlight and distracting breezes, sent instead a turbulent wind and rain which slashed across the windows. Then, too, of course there was the bother which was being made about Franklin who opened his door only to accept trays of food at appropriate hours and, although Susan assured her mother that she had nothing to fear as long as his appetite remained so excellent, Mrs. Eaton *would* fret and carry on. As for the squire, he was apparently determined not to take his son any more seriously than he had done previously and restricted his comments to such observations that if Frank were to die of a broken heart he would, at least, do so on a full stomach.

As for Susan, she kept to herself as much as possible, and was thankful that the fury of the rain kept visitors away from the house. She needed time to think and face the fact that she had allowed herself, all unaware, to become far too fond of a gentleman whose very position in life separated him from her such a distance that it was unlikely ever to be bridged, even if, as was the present case, she had proved a disappointment to him. Forever after, she knew, whenever he considered his sister's disastrous marriage, he would be reminded that had a certain Miss Eaton, whose face he would by then doubtless not remember, spoken out, all could have been prevented.

In an attempt to mitigate the pain of these reflections, Susan set out quite deliberately to disenchant herself. Indeed, she made a list of Lord Woodstone's faults, not the very least of which was his apparent inability to accept the possibility that his sister might have been in love. He had spoken of romantic nonsense and he had been cutting and hurtful in his remarks. By the time three days had run their course and the rain had finally started to abate, Susan had arrived at quite a little list of His Lordship's deficiencies, a list she read to herself at certain set hours of the day, much as though she were taking pills which, in a way, she was.

On the third day the rain slackened, revealing

roads which had become ribbons of mud which mired carriages and pedestrians with equal ease. None the less, Jane Dawson came to visit, wearing wooden pattens on her feet and carrying a large unbrella. For awhile she sat with Susan and Mrs. Eaton in the parlor talking of the weather and some few domestic problems which had occurred during their enforced separation. But, since it was clear to Susan that her friend was eager to talk about Franklin, she soon found an excuse to take her away to her bedchamber where they sat in an alcove with rain pattering on the roof overhead and spoke more intimately.

"So, he still keeps himself locked away," Jane said sadly when Susan had given her account of her brother's behavior since he had heard the news of Miss Woodstone's elopement. "I expect he will become a recluse for life."

"If Mama would do as I suggest and tell him that meals will only be served in the dining room in future, I think he might rejoin the world soon enough," Susan said dryly. "But she has always spoiled him and I do not expect she will stop, particularly since she is certain he is nursing a broken heart."

"But of course he *is*!" Jane exclaimed, flushing. "You are inclined to be too hard on him, I think."

For a moment Susan remembered how Lord Woodstone had spoken so cynically of 'romantic nonsense' and wondered if she were not being as guilty as he of lack of understanding, not to mention sympathy.

"Well, I expect he *thinks* his heart is broken, and that is nearly the same thing," she said grudgingly. "But I do wish there was something I could do to keep him from acting it all out quite so dramatically. I should think, at least, he would want to know whether Miss Woodstone has been found."

"And has she?" Jane demanded excitedly. "We have had no news since the storm began."

"No more have we," Susan told her. "I know that Lord Woodstone intended to make enquiries about Lieutenant Moore at the garrison and I believe he intended to continue his search, but the rain may have prevented it."

She had not intended to say so much, but once she had it was, of course, necessary to tell her friend about His Lordship's visit and, one thing leading to another as they tend to do, it all came out.

"So that is why you look so pale," Jane said, taking Susan's hand and pressing it. "I am so sorry that you quarreled, but you will make it up, I know."

"I doubt there will be an opportunity," Susan said in a low voice. "What little contact there was between this house and Muir Hall was only because he hoped that Maria would benefit from contact with a sensible person. That is how he thinks of me, you see. Or did. I have not even common sense to recommend me now. But do

138

not think I mind. Indeed, I have taken some pains to see the gentleman in his true colors. I only wish that you would do the same with Franklin."

"What?" Jane exclaimed. "Reckon up his faults? Why, there is no need to do so, I assure you. There has never been a time when Franklin has not been engaged passionately with one fad or another. I was fond enough of him when he thought of nothing but his telescope and when Miss Woodstone took its place in his heart I did not find him any more foolish. Or, if I did, it could be overlooked. No, my affections remain the same. He thinks of one thing at a time to the exclusion of all else, but that is his way and I would not change it."

"What a wife you would make for him!" Susan exclaimed. "Indeed, he needs someone with the patience of Job."

As Jane demurred, blushing fiercely, Betty came knocking at the door to tell Susan that there was a visitor for her in the parlor.

"It is the gentleman from Muir Hall, miss," she declared. "You must come at once, for your mama is in such a state of excitement that she is finding it difficult to make conversation."

"What! Is it Lord Woodstone!" Susan exclaimed, leaping to her feet. "For, if it is, you must tell him that I am otherwise engaged."

"No, miss. It is the other gentleman," Betty declared. "Sir Rupert Knightly."

"Well, I cannot see him either," Susan replied,

trying to mask her disappointment with a smile. "Mama must manage as best she can."

"Oh, but you cannot refuse to see him!" Jane exclaimed. "He will certainly have some news about Miss Woodstone and I do so want to know what has happened. For Franklin's sake, at least, we must keep abreast of what is going on."

Seeing her friend's dismay, Susan relented, although, she told herself, had it been Lord Woodstone, she would not have done so. Telling Betty that they would both be down in a moment, Susan took the opportunity to see that her dress was in order while Jane saw to her hair. When they passed down the corridor toward the stairs, Susan noted that Franklin's door was somewhat ajar and pointed out the fact to Jane, who grew quite pale.

"Should you not pause to speak to him?" her friend whispered.

"Indeed I will not!" Susan replied aloud. "In fact, I will take pains to close the parlor door in case he has hopes of overhearing anything which passes there. If my brother wants to know what is happening, he must make an appearance."

And, with that, she pattered down the stairs ahead of Jane to find Sir Rupert sitting opposite her mama in perfect silence, an expression of frustration on his ruddy face. As soon as the two girls entered the room, however, he leaped to his feet and made his bows, uttering the usual inanities, all of which seemed to begin with ' 'Pon my soul' and 'Damme if I don't.'

140

Shutting the door firmly behind her as she had promised, Susan put a halt to his pronouncements, most of which seemed to deal with the weather, and put the conversation on some sort of logical course by asking at once about Miss Woodstone.

"We have been a good deal concerned to know if she has been found," she said with a smile. "You know Miss Dawson, I think. Pray sit down and let us know what has been happening."

She was rewarded by grateful looks cast from three directions, Mrs. Eaton being relieved that she no longer need to attempt to find something to say, Jane being eager to learn something which might draw Franklin out of exile, and Sir Rupert being reassured that he would find a welcome, no matter what the reason.

"A bit of *on-dits*, eh?" the young gentleman exclaimed. "Nothing I'd like better, Miss Eaton. Can't tell you how good it is to get out of that house. Why, they're all as cross as crabs there and that's a fact! Makes a fellow feel like whistling down the wind!"

"It is only natural that they should be upset, surely," Susan replied. "But, tell us at once. Has Miss Woodstone been located?"

"Fleece me, but she's not Miss Woodstone any longer!" Sir Rupert declared. "Takes the name of Moore now, don't you know? Married to some lieutenant or other."

"But are you quite certain?" Susan exclaimed, while Mrs. Eaton gave a little cry.

141

"Had a letter from the jade," Sir Rupert assured her. "Posted in London. Said she was off on her honeymoon. No word as to where that was to be. Said she didn't want to be followed and argued with. Bit late for arguments, I should think, but there it is. Gel always was a goose-wit, although, mind, she can't hold a candle to my sister in *that* department!"

"Did she sound happy?" Susan asked anxiously. "I mean, did she make it clear that she went off of her own volition?"

"Said she was excessively fond of the fellow," Sir Rupert declared. "But, odd rot it, she's been excessively fond of a number of chaps, I think."

"Even so, it must be some comfort to her mother to know that she is content for the present," Susan insisted.

" 'Comfort isn't the word I'd use, nor would you if you'd been locked up in that house with Lady Woodstone for the past few days," Sir Rupert said, more lucidly than usual. "Why, to hear her talk there's no one who's ever behaved in such a shabby manner. Hole-in-the-corner. That sort of thing. Goes on day and night. Makes a fellow feel like a cat on hot bakestones, and that's a fact!'

"I expect," Mrs. Eaton ventured, "that they feel she was wrong to marry beneath her."

"That's the way of it, madam," Sir Rupert assured her. "Up or down, I say, what's the difference?"

"It's very democratic of you to say so," Susan

142

said dryly, "but I think you should not expect either Lady Woodstone or her son to agree."

"Well, as for her, she flew up into the boughs when I so much as mentioned it," Sir Rupert replied. "As for James, he made enquiries, you know. At the garrison. Discovered that Moore's a decent enough fellow. Father's a parson somewhere down near Plymouth. Nothing wrong in that."

"I hope there is not," Jane said, smiling in such a way as to make it clear to Susan just how much relief she felt to know that Maria Woodstone was no longer a threat.

"It must have come as some relief to Lord Woodstone to know something of Lieutenant Moore's background," Susan said tentatively.

" 'Pon my soul, I don't know what's in his mind," Sir Rupert told her. "He don't confide in me, at any rate. Keeps himself to himself, but I've a guess he won't be easy in his mind until he knows where his sister's got herself off to. Wants to meet the chap she's married to. Size him up. That sort of thing."

"He can do that, surely, when the lieutenant returns to duty here," Susan murmured.

"Damme, that's another twist," Sir Rupert told her. "Commander sent word yesterday that this chap Moore's sent a letter resigning his commission. What's anyone to make of that, I ask you?"

"Well, in that case, I think it careless of Lord Woodstone's sister not to tell him where she is and what her husband's plans are," Jane declared.

"Dear me!" Mrs. Eaton exclaimed, glancing at the window. "I do believe the Misses Reardon are turning in the walk. Why, they must be in a perfect frenzy for news to come out in such weather. Susan, my dear, you must call Betty to come and build up the fire for they are certain to be damp, at the very least. How pleased they will be to find you here, Sir Rupert!"

"Well, as for that, ma'am, I think I must be on my way," the young gentleman declared, rising and fairly bolting to the door. "Leave it to you to spread the news. No secret about it."

He paused to bend close to Susan who had followed him to the parlor door.

"Dash it if I hadn't set my hat on having a few words in private with you," he muttered. "It beats the Dutch how soon a crowd will gather. But I'm not one to cut my stick. Speak to you in private another time, don't you know!"

Susan smiled enigmatically and thanked him for calling, all the while making a silent resolution that such an interview as he suggested would never occur.

CHAPTER
Fourteen

Just as smiles often follow tears, the sun rose full and bright on the morning following Sir Rupert's visit. Even early on when Susan sat down to breakfast with her father the warmth was so great that they could open both the windows, letting in the tremulous birdsong and the scent of roses.

"It seems your brother does not mean to join us for still another day," the squire observed with a frown. "You know, gel, that I left him to his astronomy—though some called me a fool for doing so—because I thought there might, at least, be some future in it. But this nonsense has no redeeming value, or none that I can see. To pine away for a useless chit of a girl who has eloped with someone else seems to me to be the worst sort of folly."

"Then you must do something about it, Papa," Susan said in a spirited manner. "I have not liked to urge you before since you know your own mind in most things. I did suggest to Mama that she, at least, withhold all news of Miss Woodstone from him until he agrees to leave his room. But you know how much she pampers him. Yesterday, shen she took his dinner tray, she told him that Miss Woodstone is well and truly married, at which, she says, he seemed to fall into a decline."

"But ate his food nonetheless, I warrant," the squire said dryly.

"Only half the portions, Mama told me," Susan replied, unable to keep back a smile. "And now she is convinced that he will starve himself."

"All this is my fault," her father said with a sudden air of decision. "Willy-nilly, Frank should have taken to helping me with my business long before this. He has been idle on one excuse or other all his life, and your mama and I have put a pretty face on it. But now, I think that it is time to make a change."

"Do you mean to remove him from his chamber forcibly?" Susan demanded. "Indeed, it might be the best thing, although I am not certain."

"I must think on it," her father agreed. "Although, 'pon my soul, my impulse is to go upstairs at once and bring him out by the scruff of the neck. But I can say this, at least. Either he will see the light before this day is over, or I will take action of some sort."

"Oh, dear!" Mrs. Eaton exclaimed from the doorway where she had stood unobserved for a few moments, listening to them. "I hope you will do nothing rash, Arthur. You know how sensitive Frank is. I cannot bear to think of his being abused."

"As to that, it might be the best thing for him," her husband said gruffly, applying himself to his morning ale.

Sensing a quarrel, Susan rose and left the room to give them privacy for it. And, since it was such a fine day and she had many things to think about, she took her lightest pelisse from the hook by the door and went out into the garden. But all that she found there was too much the same as it had been the last day before the rain, when she and Lord Woodstone had talked together. As much to escape those sad memories as anything, she rounded the house and set off down the path which led to the south meadow.

At first she let herself be distracted by the sighting of the rabbits which sprang like great heaps of gray cotton in and out of their burrows. And then, there were the swooping swallows to observe and meadow flowers to gather. But, as she walked, her thoughts turned with increasing frequency to her troubles until she drifted on an uncharted course across the meadow, lost in her mind's eye.

How foolish she had been to think that she could escape thoughts of Lord Woodstone simply be leaving the shelter of the garden. And yet, what had happened had happened. Time and again she reminded herself that it did no good to go over what they had said to one another, word for word. His sister was married and, if she had spoken, she might have prevented it. How like her it had been yesterday to try to wrench from Sir Rupert some assurance that Maria was happy. As though, in Lord Woodstone's and his mother's eyes, that would solve anything! In desperation, Susan resorted to reciting silently the list of Lord Woodstone's faults and then, calling herself a fool, gave up trying a persuasion which found no soil to root itself in.

Well then, she told herself, if the day would not serve to distract, and lists do nothing to dissuade, then she must turn to other troubles. There was Franklin, of course, but all that she felt on conjuring up thoughts on her brother was such frustration at his foolishness that she would like to strike out at something. Even if her father were to remove him from his bedchamber by force or lure him out by withholding food, he would have not changed. What was wanted was something which would bring about a change in character or, although she dared not hope for it, prove that he had hidden strengths which thus far he had seen fit to keep a secret. How, she wondered, could Jane Dawson love him? Oh, it was true that he was gentle and intelligent when

148

it came to bookish matters. She herself loved him well enough, despite his silly ways, but that was because she was his sister. With Jane it must be different.

And then it came to her that she was refuting the very arguments she had made to herself in the case of Maria Woodstone. Her match with the young officer might seem to others to be a giddy act, but, as she herself had reminded Lord Woodstone, Maria was human and might well feel genuine affection. There was no reason behind love, and she had been angry with him when he had spoken of romantic nonsense. She had tried to defend herself by making a display of pragmatism, by offering practical advice. But had she spoken truthfully she would have defended Maria's right to love whom she chose. And now she was twisting what she believed, wondering why Jane should care for Franklin, asking for reasons. Who should know better than she who had made a list to prove it that the heart did not follow always to its best advantage?

And here she was back at Lord Woodstone again! Her mind seemed quite incapable of moving in anything but circles. Breaking into a run, Susan felt the fresh breeze on her flushed face. It gave her some relief and she did not stop until she was breathless and her bonnet was hanging by its ribbon on her back. Pausing by an ancient beech tree which stood in the very center of the meadow and which her father had preserved for its beauty, she looked to east and west to reassure herself that no one had seen her wild behavior. It was one thing to have run here as a child as she had so often done, and quite another to have anyone observe a young lady darting through the grass like one possessed. And, as she looked, Susan caught sight of two figures standing very close together in the knoll which bordered on the grounds of Muir Hall. Her eyes were sharp and even though they were at a distance, Susan saw that it was the Misses Reardon's Patience and Lord Woodstone's footman Tom, and that they were just done embracing.

Susan started to stroll away at once, not wanting them to know they had been seen. But in a moment she heard her name being called and, looking back, saw Patience hurrying after her, Tom having disappeared.

"Miss Eaton!" Patience declared breathlessly when she was still some distance away. "Do wait, miss! Happens I've been wanting to have a word with you in private like."

Susan pretended to be surprised at the meeting, but Patience gave a pert smile which made it clear that she was undeceived.

"You've seen me meeting Tom, I expect," she said, pushing her curls more securely under her mobcap.

Confronted with such honesty, Susan admitted that she had.

"Every morning when I go to fetch eggs at Farmer Longley's, I make a detour like," the girl said laughing and patting the basket on her arm.

"It's a way of mine to mix a little pleasure with the business of the day."

Her good humor was so infectious that Susan found herself giving assurances that she would say nothing of the meeting to Patience's two elderly mistresses.

"Why, as to that, miss, I think they would not mind so much if they only knew how much warm gossip I bring back with their eggs. Happens they're so fond of both—the eggs and gossip, I mean—that they would be more than willing to overlook a tiny indiscretion here or there."

Knowing the Misses Reardon, Susan hazarded a guess that what Patience said might well be true.

"Still, I will say nothing," she declared. "After all, it is no one's business but your own, and no fault of yours that I happened to be wandering this way."

"Well, it was not that I wanted to talk to you about, miss," Patience told her. "The fact is that Tom and me's been engaging in a little argument."

Susan did not suggest that it was probably not such a disagreeable disagreement if the warmth of their embrace was any proof, although she thought it.

"As soon as I caught sight of you, I told him straight," Patience went on. " 'There's Miss Eaton,' I said. 'She'll tell us what's right to do, she being such a sensible sort.' "

The words made Susan wince, remembering who last had called her sensible and then had reason to regret it.

"I will give you what advice I can," Susan said, knowing that she would seem condescending if she were to say otherwise. "But you must not count on it overmuch. I make as many mistaken judgments as others, and sometimes, I think more."

"Well, as for that, miss," Patience declared, "I have never heard your mistakes spoken of and if I do not hear a thing I have some cause to doubt it, for, as you know, my ears are very sharp."

"Ah, yes," Susan said thoughtfully. "It was you who brought the news that Miss Woodstone had eloped, I think."

"That it was," Patience said proudly. "All thanks to Tom, that was. You've heard perhaps she's gone and married, miss. But then, of course you have, for when I told the mistresses nothing would keep them in the house until they had spread the word about the village. Talk about damp petticoats! They're airing still by the kitchen fire. But there! I've fetched myself away from my own point, though as it has to do with Miss Woodstone what was there's no harm in it."

"Is there more word from her, then?" Susan asked, feeling her blood begin to race, which was the effect, it seemed, that any news from Muir Hall was destined to have on her now.

"This time it's me who knows a thing or two to tell Tom," Patience said happily. "Just a bit of

152

information I stored away in the back of my mind like. Sorting and ordering the other day I happened to come on it. Something I overheard, you understand, and put no importance on at the time. Still, as I say, one stores away all sorts of bits of information."

"Yes, yes," Susan said impatiently, thinking how garrulous the spreading of gossip was making the little maid. "And what did you remember?"

"Why, the very name of the place those two are making their honeymoon at, I warrant," Patience told her with an air of satisfaction.

"What! Miss Woodstone and the lieutenant?"

"Just so, miss. They were taking tea at the Misses Reardon's one afternoon, you understand. Chatting by themselves in the corner like. And, as I was passing around cakes and such . . ."

"You eavesdropped," Susan suggested to bring her to the point.

"It is a habit of mine," Patience admitted. "One I've been encouraged to develop, if you please, miss."

"I understand," Susan assured her. "But what precisely did you hear?"

"Why, miss, only the lieutenant—a lovely gentleman to my way of thinking, with hair like a baby's—the lieutenant was talking of a place on the seashore he was very fond of. How he was going on about the waves and such! I declare I could almost see it myself. And Miss Woodstone looking at him with her eyes ever so wide. My,

153

but they made a handsome couple to my way of thinking!"

"Yes, yes," Susan urged her.

"Well, and then she said how she would like to see it, and he whispered something ever so low and she began to giggle."

"And was that all?" Susan said disappointedly.

"Why, miss, I heard the name of the place, and that's the important thing. Studley-by-the-Sea. That was it exactly. And, as I say, I pushed it back into my mind and . . ."

"Have you told this to Tom?" Susan interrupted.

"That was what we was arguing about, miss," Patience said blandly. "He's of the opinion that if the young lady wants to remain out of the way for a bit, that's her privilege. But it's my way of thinking that the family should know. Or, at least Lord Woodstone."

"And I think that you are right," Susan told her. "Lord Woodstone knows the marriage cannot be prevented now. But it is understandable that he would want to know where his sister is. Whether he would go to her must be his decision, but I think that you should tell him what you have told me and as soon as possible."

"La, but I couldn't do that, miss!" Patience exclaimed. "I wouldn't dare. I'm very well with the ladies in the village, you understand. They know my ways and I know theirs. But there's a difference when it comes to nobs and such!"

"Well, then, Tom must tell his master," Susan insisted.

"He will not do it, miss. I've made myself hoarse trying to convince him. But it would be easy enough for you to do it, being acquainted with the gentleman and all."

Susan's first instinct was to protest. But then she made herself pause and think. She had failed Lord Woodstone once. Nothing could help that. But she would always blame herself if she did not let him know what Patience had told her. Angry as they had been when they had parted last, she could do this last favor, at least.

"Very well," she said. "I will return home and write a note."

"It would be easier to tell him at once, miss, if you'll pardon the suggestion," Patience said. "He's at home this morning. Tom told me that he was. And it's no more than a ten-minute walk to the house from here."

"Oh, very well," Susan said, thinking only that the sooner it was over and done, the sooner she would feel her debt to Lord Woodstone dispatched. Perhaps then she could have some peace of mind. And, as Patience said, the distance was so slight.

"It's a good deed you're doing, miss, I'm sure of it. You'll find His Lordship in the garden. Tom said he was out there making plans to put it all in order. A bit glum, like, Tom said. But that's to be understood, isn't it? When he hears

155

what you've come to tell him, he'll be in a better temper, I've no doubt."

"Well, if he is or isn't, I don't care," Susan muttered to herself as she struck off across the field. "At least he'll have his last bit of information from me. And that will put a period to it all."

CHAPTER
Fifteen

The Muir estate had once been bounded all entirely by a stone wall some nine feet in height and covered at the top with bits of glass stuck points out with cement as though to keep a rabid countryside at bay. The present owner, however, being of a more trusting nature and often away, to boot, had not seen to it that repairs in the encircling structure were attended to, with the result that in a good many places the stones had succumbed to time and weather; with a certain leveling consequently taking place at various spots. Thus it was that Susan found it quite unnecessary to approach the manor house from its grand entry drive; being able, instead, to slip directly into the rose garden by the simple expediency of stepping over a crumbled ledge of rocks.

The garden and, indeed, the grounds of Muir Hall were quite familiar to her. Because of the owner's prolonged absences, she had often as a child, with her brother and others from the village, come here to play. The last time she had set foot in this garden had, however, been some years ago and now she stood and looked about her at the broken sundial and the tangled clumps of rosebushes with the sense of having somehow stepped back in time. How vastly different life had been then, she reflected. How uncomplicated and untroubled it all seemed, looked at from a distance. She could almost hear the childish voices of herself and her companions as they had played their noisy games. Closing her eyes she drank in the scent of the roses, made even sweeter by their wildness. She would be sad, she thought, to see it all set to order with the graveled paths well marked and clipped along the edge and the rosebeds made neat with piles of loam.

But, she reminded herself, there was no time for idle musings of this sort. She was on an errand of a serious nature and one which was certain, at the very least, to be awkward. She must deliver her message and depart as soon as possible and if this was the last time she would see the garden, then that was as it must be. At least in coming here for one final visit, she might put her mind to rest. Once Lord Woodstone was told, she could forget him, for then she would owe him nothing.

But as she made her way through the wilderness of roses with the long windows of the Hall itself peering down at her, she discovered that, despite what Patience had told her, Lord Woodstone was nowhere in sight. But the garden was vast and the bushes so high that she could not see everywhere at once and so she wandered, looking to the right and left, stopping frequently to free the muslin of her gown from the clasp of thorns.

And then, turning a corner banked with scarlet roses which seemed to elbow one another to catch a glimpse of the sun, she came upon Drusella Knightly. The girl was kneeling on the ground, making a vain attempt to catch a toad. Sensing no doubt that she was observed, she sprang to her feet and covered her mouth with both hands.

Susan had never been certain what attitude to take to this peculiar young lady. On the one hand she thought she might be simple and, if so, to be pitied. But, on the other hand, her manner might be accounted for by ordinary rudeness. At all events, she was not particularly pleased to find her here. It was awkward. More than that, it was embarrassing, for what was she but an uninvited guest making free with the garden? In as cool a manner as she could manage, Susan announced that she was looking for Lord Woodstone, and that she had brought a message.

At once Drusella broke into a fit of giggles and Susan was reminded of the several other instances when she had seen the girl react in the same manner. Was it nerves, she wondered, or simple amusement at some long extended private joke?

"I had reason to think that His Lordship was occupied here in the garden," Susan said evenly. "Perhaps you can tell me if he is about."

Keeping her mouth covered with one hand and continuing to shake with laughter, Drusella pointed to the left and then proceeded to follow her own finger with lightning speed, soon disappearing beyond a tangle of bushes.

How she was to interpret this strange behavior Susan did not know. She only hoped that Drusella meant to indicate that Lord Woodstone was to be found in the direction she had indicated and, with this as her only clue, Susan proceeded accordingly. But ten minutes later, having reached the further boundary of the garden without seeing anyone, she admitted defeat. Cursing herself silently for having come here, she proceeded to make her way back to the wall by the most direct route. But, of course, she should have sent a note. How absurd it had been for her to have taken Patience's suggestion in the first place.

And then, quite suddenly, she found her way barred by a shadow and, looking up, found Sir Rupert Knightly standing directly in her path. A broad smile threatened to cleave his wide face in two as he stepped toward her and bowed with a sort of mock formality which put her instantly on guard.

"What a pleasant surprise, Miss Eaton!" he exclaimed. "I had thought that I would have to come to you for our private talk. How delightful to discover that I have been anticipated."

"I am here to see Lord Woodstone on a matter of business," Susan said with all the dignity that she could manage in the situation. "I met your sister here a few minutes ago and she seemed to indicate that he was somewhere about."

"Yes, yes. Quite so," Sir Rupert replied. "I think he may have just stepped in the house for a few minutes, but he is certain to be back directly. Dash it, the fellow's at work night and day about this place, though what's the use of it when you can hire others I'm damned if I know."

Susan looked at him suspiciously, taking two steps backward so that they would not stand so close together.

"Perhaps your sister told you that I was here," she suggested.

"Perhaps she did! Perhaps she did! That's for me to know, Miss Eaton, and you to find out. Drusella's a bit dim at times, you know, but that's not to mean she doesn't know a thing or two."

"I don't know what you mean by that, sir," Susan said. "At all events, I think that, after all, I will not wait. It will be best to send a note, I think."

"But you cannot think of leaving me so abruptly," Sir Rupert declared, at the same time making it impossible to do so by stepping forward in such a way that she was backed against a thornbush. " 'Pon my soul, I meant it when I said that we should have a word or two in private."

Susan was aware of a momentary sense of fear. Sir Rupert was not as tall as Lord Woodstone, but he was massively built. If she were to try to rush past him and he to stop her, there was no question that she should struggle in vain. And she did not want it to come to that. The situation was already undignified enough. What a complete idiot she had been to entertain Patience's proposal that she come here!

"You are standing in my way, sir," she said in as even a voice as she could muster. "I wish to leave now and I will be grateful to you if you will permit me to do so."

Sir Rupert laughed.

"Why, it is only shyness on your part, Miss Eaton," he assured her. " 'Pon my soul, there's no harm in our having a little tête-à-tête. Said you wanted to see Woodstone, didn't you? Fellow's bound to turn up in a few minutes. Damme, if you've come on business, he won't half turn havey-cavey if he finds out I've let you fly the coop."

"I have already told you that I have decided to send him a message," Susan said icily. Anger had shouldered trepidation to one side and she was in complete control of herself again. "I do not think that Lord Woodstone would like to hear that you had kept me here against my will. But, if you do not let me go quietly, that is precisely what I will tell him."

"What do I care what Woodstone likes or don't like?" Sir Rupert demanded. "Perhaps you think I could not hold my own with him, eh? Why, if it should come to a bout of fisticuffs, I should welcome the opportunity. Too sure of himself by half he is, and no mistake. Never would have come here in the first place if my mother hadn't got the notion into her head that she could make a match between him and my sister."

The thought of Lord Woodstone making an offer for the tittering Drusella was so absurd that, for a moment, Susan was distracted.

"A goose-witted idea that was," Sir Rupert went on. "Almost as addlepated as her idea that I make a bid for Maria. Why, that gel was nothing but a pea-goose. Told Her Ladyship that at the start, and you see how events have born me out. Dash it, I like a bit of sense in a gel, damned if I don't! Sense and spirit, that's the combination."

The conversation—if one could call it that— had, Susan saw, drifted into dangerous waters. She would have had to be far more naive than she was to misinterpret the look in Sir Rupert's eyes.

"Let me pass," she said again in a low voice.

"Playing coy don't suit you, miss," he told her. "No need for games, in any case. Oh, I know how ladies like to lead a fellow on and then draw back a bit. Fashionable thing to do, eh? But you and me, Miss Eaton, we can talk straight out. No need to bandy words."

"I am not playing a game," Susan said, furious now. "Whatever you may believe, sir, I have no intention of being coy. I find this conversation distasteful. I do not wish to remain here with you. And, if I bandy words with anyone, it will not be with you!"

"Now, don't pretend you haven't flirted with me in the past," Sir Rupert declared. "It won't do, I assure you."

"Flirted!" Susan exclaimed. "That is absurd, sir!"

"I know a thing or two about ladies," Sir Rupert said ponderously. "Don't think I've had no opportunity for experience."

"Perhaps you have, sir, but not with me!" Susan told him, clenching her hands. "Now, will you let me pass?"

"Not until I've had my say," Sir Rupert told her. "No doubt you think I mean to trifle with your affections. Perfectly understandable if you did. After all, there is my rank to consider and what are you, after all, but a country squire's daughter? That's it, isn't it? You think I mean to make a toy of your affections."

"That would be impossible, sir," Susan assured

164

him. "You could never engage my affections, in the first place. Indeed, since you have forced me to be candid, let me assure you that I feel nothing for you at the moment but the most extreme aversion."

"Spirit!" Sir Rupert exclaimed. "Told you I liked a bit of spirit, didn't I? Good of you to make a little display to oblige. Damned clever, too."

Rage and frustration made Susan want to scream. Indeed, she would have done so if she had not wanted quite so desperately to avoid further unpleasantness. Was there nothing she could say to convince this singularly unpleasant man that he meant nothing to her? She could not move or he would restrain her by force. Of that she was quite certain. And, if he was given the excuse to touch her, what would come of it? She could think of nothing to do but resort to a straight insult. Angry, he might forget his obviously amorous intentions.

"I think you are a fool, sir," she said clearly. "And a bounder, as well."

"What's this?" Sir Rupert demanded. "You go beyond the boundary of coyness, Miss Eaton, damme if you don't!"

"It is you who have insisted on this conversation," Susan told him. "You force me to listen to you and now you will listen to me. I found you a bore from the first moment I met you. If you have ever said an amusing word, I have not

165

heard it. Your person is not agreeable to me in any way. Shall I become more particular?"

"Dash it, aren't you doing it a bit brown?" Sir Rupert said, having the good grace to look genuinely bemused. "No doubt you only mean to have your bit of fun. To tease a bit. But you go too far, Miss Eaton. I will not be made a cake of!"

"Then let me go!" Susan demanded. "If you do not, you shall hear a few more home truths, I assure you. Enough, I fancy, to convince you that I am no tease."

"Come now, you know you fancy me," Sir Rupert said in rough voice. "No need to draw away from me like that. Intentions honorable, and all that sort of thing. Mean to offer for you, if you'll let me get a word in edgewise, and that's a fact. Set the village on its ears, we will, my little lovely."

And, as Susan stared at him, appalled, he reached out for her. In an instant she was struggling in his bear-like embrace. Only by dint of twisting and turning was she able to keep him from kissing her.

"Ah, yes, you fancy me," she heard him mutter as he pressed her to him in a vise-like grip. Her face was pressed against his shoulder. She could not cry out or make a sound. But her eyes were clear. And, with a sense of horror, she found herself looking straight into Lord Woodstone's face.

For a moment he paused and an extraordinary

expression which she could not decipher came into his dark, hooded eyes. And then, turning on his heel, he was gone as suddenly as he had come.

CHAPTER
Sixteen

An hour later, locked in her chamber as securely as her brother was locked in his, Susan raged in silence. What had happened was not her fault and yet she knew she would be blamed for it. Clenching her hands into fists and pressing them against her eyes, she remembered the look in Lord Woodstone's eyes. A relentless dismay possessed her, as it had in that awful moment. She did not know now how she had managed to pull herself from Sir Rupert's loathsome embrace. She did remember pushing past him and running, running, not daring to look behind her to see if he were following. She had only really come to herself when she had reached the further side of the south meadow. Only then had she looked back and, in her utter relief at seeing nothing but the swaying grass, sunk down

169

into its fragrant softness and hugged her misery close to her.

How much time then passed she did not know, but when, at last, she rose and hurried the rest of the way home, her father and her mother were at luncheon.

"They are both asking after you, miss," Sally whispered as she met Susan coming through the door. "La, whatever has happened to you?"

Glancing down at her wrinkled, grass-stained gown, Susan realized what a sight she must make. There was no question of going in to join her parents in such a state. They would ask questions, questions which she was far too rattled to answer.

"You must tell them that I walked rather further than I meant to and . . . and that I am very tired," she murmured to the little maid. "Say that the sun was too hot and I have a slight headache. I mean to take a nap directly. Say that. Say anything. But see to it that I am left alone!"

Now, two hours later, she knew that Sally must have made a good story of it for, although she had heard her mother's footsteps earlier outside her door and heard the pause as well that meant she listened for a moment, Susan had been undisturbed, no doubt because she was thought to be sleeping.

But sleep was the furthest thing from Susan's mind. Indeed she wondered if she could ever rest again. How cruel it had been of Sir Rupert to have placed her in such a compromising situation! What could Lord Woodstone have thought but that she had arranged a rendezvous with his guest, had been so bold, in fact, as to meet the gentleman in his own garden! Worse than that, he would think her wanton! What other possible conclusion could he have reached?

If only Sir Rupert had not held her so tightly! If only Lord Woodstone could have seen that she was attempting to struggle! She tried to visualize the scene as he had come upon it. Thinking himself alone, he had turned a corner and seen her in what appeared to be a passionate embrace. Even his own sister would not have been so indiscreet! What *must* he think of her! Oh, it was cruel, cruel!

Would he mention what he had seen to Sir Rupert? That was the next tormenting thought to come to mind. And if he did, what answer would his guest make? Sir Rupert had declared himself. He had seemed to think that she was being coy, despite the manner in which she had insulted him. The man was so self-centered, so obtuse that doubtless he had not realized that she meant everything she had said quite literally. And, if so, would he tell Lord Woodstone that there was, indeed, a love match between them? She did not know what would be worse, to have Lord Woodstone believe that she could ever entertain even the slightest affection for such a frightful man or that she was engaged in a frivolous flirtation.

It did not bear thinking of! And yet she could think of nothing else. How ironic it was that she had gone to Muir Hall instead of sending a message for the express purpose of relieving her mind. And now, instead, she had burdened it to such a degree that it almost seemed she could not bear it.

When the tap came at her door, Susan realized that she had not bothered to change her dress and that the hours spent pacing back and forth across the room or huddled on the bed had done little to improve her appearance. So it was that she did not open the door but simply called to ask who was there.

"It's Sally, miss," the answer came. "Do let me in."

Well, Sally had seen her as she was when she had arrived home and it could do little harm to let her see her now. Besides, she could be trusted, Susan told herself, as she turned the key.

"Oh, Miss, you must be in such dreadful trouble," the girl declared as she came into the room. "And yet downstairs they are saying . . ."

"Who is saying what?" Susan demanded.

"The Misses Reardon are in the sitting room with your mother, miss, and Mrs. Jackson and her daughters have just joined them as well. And there is such excitement! Your mother is all in a tremble, miss, and could not come to fetch you herself. But I think you must go down at once and make an explanation!"

"But what should I explain?" Susan said. "Come. Make yourself clearer, Sally, do!"

"They are saying that you have engaged yourself to Sir Rupert Knightly, miss," Sally said hesitantly. "The news came from the Hall."

"By way of Patience, I assume," Susan said grimly. "It is all a mistake, Sally. There is no truth in it."

"Well, you must go down then and tell them so," the little maid insisted. "Your mother is quite beside herself to think that you would promise yourself to anyone without her knowing a word of it."

"Has Papa heard this?" Susan demanded.

"No, miss. He went to Tunburg straight after luncheon on business."

"Thanks for that at least," Susan said with a sigh. "Oh, poor Mama! What a monster that man is! But you are right. I must set Mama's mind at ease at once, and put a stop to the gossip before it is spread all over the village. Help me with this frock, Sally. Yes, I will exchange it for the blue sprigged muslin. And pour some water in the bowl so that I can wash my face. And find my brush. My hair must be in quite a frightful state!"

Not ten minutes later Susan descended the stairs, her slim shoulders squared as one who approaches an arena. A silence fell on the company as she crossed the threshold of the sitting room. And then her mother cried, "Oh, Susan! Is it true?"

"Is what true, Mama?" Susan replied, deciding that feigning innocence of the matter under discussion would serve her best. "Good afternoon,

Miss Reardon. Good afternoon, Miss Reardon. How nice to see you Mrs. Jackson. And Ruth and Priscilla, too. What a pleasant surprise to find such a company waiting."

And they *were* waiting. That was clear enough. Indeed, Ruth and Priscilla sat, quite literally, on the edges of their seats.

"Oh, my dear!" Mrs. Eaton continued. "The Misses Reardon have brought me such astonishing news that I cannot bring myself to believe it!"

"Why then," Susan said with a display of calmness which she did not feel, "Patience must have been particularly busy."

She was not accustomed to flinging barbs, at least not in the direction of the two maiden ladies, but underneath her cool exterior her temper was beginning to rage. The speed with which gossip flew about the village had often annoyed her before, but now that it concerned her private affairs she found it intolerable.

Miss Martha flushed and Miss Willamena grew very pale.

"Granted that Patience was our source," the former said, "but we would not have seen fit to repeat it if she had not so often proved to be correct."

"And if what she told us not an hour ago is true, then of course it follows that we should be the first to offer our felicitations," Miss Willamena added.

"Felicitations?" Susan said, taking a chair and

174

sitting very upright in it, her hands clasped neatly in her lap. "It is good news, then?"

"It cannot be true, my dear," her mother wailed. "I have just been saying that surely you would have told me before the entire village came to know of it."

"Then may I take it that this news concerns me?" Susan said with a sweetness she was far from feeling. "That comes as a surprise, I assure you, for I can think of nothing which has happened to me of a nature to arouse public curiosity."

Even while she spoke her mind was busy. Never, if she could prevent it, would she allow her mother to hear of how she had been embarrassed that morning. Whatever gossip Patience had gathered must have come from Tom. How much he had been able to tell her Susan was not certain. She could only hope that Lord Woodstone had said nothing of what he had seen in the garden. Surely the precise nature of the event was not something that Sir Rupert would brag about.

"Why, now, is it not true, child, that Sir Rupert Knightly has offered for you and that you have accepted?" Mrs. Jackson exclaimed.

"What an absurd notion," Susan said evenly. "I am afraid that this time Patience has failed you all."

"I knew it must be false!" Mrs. Eaton cried. "Oh, my dear, I am that relieved!"

"How can you say that when it would have

175

made such a handsome match for Susan?" Mrs. Jackson demanded. "Why if it had been Ruth or Priscilla . . ."

"I cannot understand it," Miss Martha said, knitting her forehead in perplexity. "Patience was quite positive about it."

"Perhaps she told you when this offer was presumed to have been made," Susan said carefully.

"Why, as to that, I do not know. She only said that one of the servants at the Hall who is a friend of hers had told her that Sir Rupert announced it to his mother and the others this morning. She was told, as well, that there was considerable excitement there."

Miss Willamena spoke quickly and pursed her lips when she had finished in a way that made Susan certain that 'excitement' had not been the word Patience had used. Indeed, she could imagin the dismay with which Lady Knightly must have received the information that her only son was to marry a squire's daughter.

"Excitement," Susan mused. "Ah, yes. And were there no other details to embellish this amusing story?"

"Why, no. That was all, I think," Miss Martha said. "I should have said it was quite enough!"

Lord Woodstone had not spoken, then! Inwardly, Susan breathed a sigh of relief. He had guarded her reputation by not mentioning that he had seen the embrace. That, in itself, was something, although it did nothing to cancel the fact that he must believe what Sir Rupert had told him and the others. There could be no doubt in his mind that she had affianced herself, and that with unbecoming lack of modesty. Still, she must not think of that. Indeed, she could not, for the pain was too great. She must take one step at a time, and that quite carefully. The great thing now was to convince her mother and the others that the news had no basis in fact.

"But why would anyone have told Patience this if it were not true?" Miss Martha puzzled.

"Perhaps Sir Rupert declared that he was affianced to someone and Patience's source misheard the name," Susan suggested. "It is the only answer I can think of. But, let me add this. Had Sir Rupert offered, I would never have accepted. The gentleman is a bore at best and perhaps, I think, a scoundrel. You will all be doing me a great favor if this is not mentioned elsewhere. In fact, it would please me very well if we spoke no more of it from this moment on."

"Of course, my dear," Miss Martha murmured.

"I shall have a sharp word with Patience," Miss Willamena added.

"It is all such a disappointment," Mrs. Jackson said. "But there. You need not scowl at me so, Susan. That is my last word on the subject."

"And we will be as quiet as the grave," Ruth Jackson said. "Is that not correct, Priscilla?"

"La, it will take an effort, but we will," her sister echoed.

"Then let us all take a cup of tea," Susan suggested. "Dear Mama! You must calm yourself now. If ever I become affianced, you will be the first to know."

CHAPTER
Seventeen

By the time Jane Dawson arrived at the Eaton house, Mrs. Jackson and her daughters, together with the Misses Reardon, having been duly offered tea and cake, were being ushered out by Susan whose smile, as Jane was quick to note, had a strained quality about it.

"I am sure they mean well," Susan muttered to her friend as soon as the door was closed behind them, "but, I declare, sometimes I think that they will drive me to distraction."

"They would strain the patience of a saint," Jane agreed. "And, as for meaning well, I think you are too generous. What gossip have they been spreading this afternoon?"

Susan could not wait to tell her, but first she

found it necessary to return to the sitting room to reassure her mother once again.

"Now, take a little doze on the sofa, Mama, do," she murmured. "Jane and I will visit in my room upstairs. And mind, not a word of this to Papa. It would only upset him, and all so unnecessarily. I declare I wish that you had never heard it."

Mrs. Eaton, having agreed to settle on the sofa with a crocheted shawl wrapped about her, the two girls hurried up the stairs at such a rate that, on reaching the landing, they were in time to see Franklin's door being hastily drawn closed.

"Did you see that?" Jane whispered as they went into Susan's room. "What does it mean?"

"It means his curiosity is still alive, at any rate," Susan said thoughtfully. "I wonder just how much he heard."

And with that by way of introduction, she proceeded to inform her friend precisely what had happened that afternoon.

"But how could Patience have come by such a story?" Jane declared when Susan had finished. "I have never known her to be wrong before. You know that she is walking out with that footman from the Hall. I'm certain that she gets her information from him. Why would he have told her such a Banbury tale?"

"Well, there *is* a degree of truth in it," Susan murmured, curling up on the bed while Jane took the window seat. "Promise you will tell no one."

"But of course I promise."

Whereupon Susan recounted the morning's events in some detail, only leaving out the part about Lord Woodstone having come upon her and Sir Rupert. That, she found, she could not bear to tell, even to her dearest friend. It was something she must try to forget as soon as possible and that would be easiest accomplished if no one knew.

"But what a rake the fellow is!" Jane exclaimed excitedly. "Why, this is frightful, Susan! He should be called out, indeed he should."

"Papa might do so if he knew," Susan replied. "But neither you nor I will ever tell him and there is no other way he could come to know of it that I can think of."

"But if Sir Rupert has told his mother that he is engaged, you cannot hope to hear the last of it," Jane reminded her. "Doubtlessly the next thing that will happen is that he will appear here and ask to see your father to make a formal request for your hand. Clearly he did not believe you when you refused him."

"There is that," Susan said thoughtfully. "I have been so upset that I could not think clearly of what might happen next. Well, if he comes I will make certain Papa is prepared. I will tell him . . ."

"Yes?" Jane encouraged her when she paused.

"I will be very vague about it," Susan went on hesitantly. "I will say that I have reason to think that Sir Rupert might offer and that, if he comes to Papa, he is to tell him that he cannot consent to the proposal. That should put an end to that. The Misses Reardon have promised not to repeat the story and Mrs. Jackson and her daughters, too."

"But, surely, knowing them you cannot possibly believe . . ."

"They promised," Susan repeated stubbornly. "Besides, I convinced them that it was not true and you know what great stock they put on being right. Certainly they will not risk their reputation for only spreading valid gossip."

"No doubt you are right," Jane said. 'We must be hopeful, at all events. Yes, the worst that can happen now is that Sir Rupert will arrive to see your father. And, as you say, if he is prepared to deal with him . . ."

She broke off to utter an exclaimation which reflected so much alarm that Susan echoed it involuntarily.

"Oh dear!" Jane cried, pointing out the window. "Oh dear! Only come and see who is arriving at your front gate!"

Springing from the bed, Susan joined her friend and, looking down, saw to her horror that Lady Woodstone and Lady Knightly were stepping out of a carriage, assisted by Ned Barstow from Handley who had taken the position of groom at Muir Hall. A great business was subsequently made of holding up skirts and petticoats as though the walk to the squire's door was a mire of mud instead of a path of neat bricks.

Despite the fact that both ladies wore high poke bonnets, elaborately laced at the edges, Susan could see that very grim looks indeed were being displayed, with the result that even the most casual passerby, had there been one, could have seen at once that this was not an ordinary afternoon call.

"This is the last thing I expected!" Susan exclaimed, pressing both hands to her cheeks. "They intend to make a scene. I am certain of it. I will call down to Sally to tell them that no one is at home to receive them."

"There is no time," Jane told her, having pushed the casement open to give her a better view as the two ladies approached the house. "They are already knocking. And, yes, Sally has opened the door. They are asking for your mother."

"Poor Mama!" Susan cried. "She has already endured enough because of me for one day. First the Misses Reardon and Mrs. Jackson, and now this!"

"Listen to me," Jane declared, taking her arm. "I will hurry downstairs and receive them in the back parlor. Sally will be dithering about whether or not to disturb your mother in the sitting room. She *is* napping, is she not?"

"Yes! Yes! Take them to the parlor," Susan exclaimed. "I will be down to relieve you directly. Only be certain to tell Sally that Mama is to be allowed to sleep. With any luck they will have gone by the time she wakes."

Jane was out of the room before Susan had spoken the last word. Susan heard her slippered feet on the stairs and a creaking noise which alerted her to the fact that Franklin must be eavesdropping again. Well, let him listen all he liked, she told herself. This time she would make no effort to keep him from hearing. It was one thing to keep her mother from knowing of the difficulties which had beset the household, and quite another to permit him to keep his head in the sand like an ostrich.

Minutes later, when she had tied her hair for a second time and smoothed her muslin gown, Susan hurried down the stairs, pretending not to notice Franklin's belated attempts to close his door. He would, she knew, open it again as soon as she was out of sight.

Jane had been as good as her word. Sally waited anxiously before the closed door to the sitting room and the two visitors were out of sight, if not of sound, since Susan could hear their high voices being raised in the back parlor.

"We must hope that Mama sleeps as soundly as usual today," Susan whispered to the little maid. "But, mind you, if she should awake, see to it that she does not interrupt us. Use any excuse. There is no time for me to think of any."

"Oh, miss, they seemed so angry!" Sally told her. "Like two twin dragons, I declare!"

"I will play St. George to them," Susan assured her with a confidence she was far from feeling. "Only do your part and I will do mine."

And, with that, she was off down the hall, bracing herself so that she should enter the parlor with as much dignity as she could muster, and found Lady Woodstone and Lady Knightly sitting side by side on the sofa, staring coldly at Jane who was attempting to make some explanation of who she was and why Mrs. Eaton had not received them.

"My mother is resting," Susan said by way of announcing herself. "She did not expect visitors this afternoon, and she has had a number of them already."

Two bonneted heads swiveled toward her. Two narrow noses poked themselves in her direction. Two pairs of beady eyes examined her with no pretense of cordiality.

"You have made us a brusque welcome, Miss Eaton," Lady Woodstone said accusingly.

"It is her country ways," Lady Knightly said in an undertone.

"Yes, it is my country way," Susan replied. "No doubt in London some pretense would be made of friendships which do not exist. But I prefer to be more direct. I doubt you care any more than I to linger about this business."

"There is no doubt in her mind why we have come, Regina," Lady Knightly hissed. "You see that she intends to defy us."

"You have come about Sir Rupert," Susan said evenly. "And if by defy you mean that I intend to oppose your wishes, you are quite mistaken."

185

"You speak in riddles, Miss Eaton," Lady Woodstone said coldly.

"There is no riddle about the purpose of your visit, madam," Susan replied quickly. "And I have stated it as directly as I know how. Shall I repeat myself? You have come about Sir Rupert."

"Yes, that is quite true," Lady Woodstone said shrilly. "I feel a certain responsibility about what has happened since my friend, Lady Knightly, came to Muir Hall in all innocence."

"May I ask in innocence of what?" Susan demanded, glancing a warning at Jane not to interrupt.

"Why, indeed you may, my girl," Lady Woodstone said condescendingly. "When I pressed my invitation, I did not warn her that there were scheming jades to be found here in this village, chits who would take any means at their disposal to ensnare any gentleman who sports a title."

"By that you mean Lady Knightly's son, I expect," Susan replied. "You see, I have heard indirectly something of the matter, but I would prefer to listen to you state it straight out."

"Such vulgarity!" Lady Knightly murmured, fetching a vinaigrette from her reticule and pressing it to her nose.

"If that is what you care to call the direct approach, madam, then that is your privilege, Susan retorted. "Come, Lady Woodstone. Who are these chits and jades you speak of?"

Lady Woodstone took a deep breath. "Why,

there is only one, Miss Eaton," she said in such a penetrating voice that Susan could only hope her mother's sleep was as sound as she supposed. "Only one, and that is you. You have enticed this lady's only son. But we have come to tell you that we intend to bring him to his senses before further damage is done."

"Why, as to bringing Sir Rupert to his senses, the sooner you can do it, the better," Susan replied. "From what I have seen of him, however, that will be an awesome undertaking."

Lady Woodstone braced herself as though a hot poker had been applied to her back. "I cannot think what it is you mean to tell us, Miss Eaton!" she declared.

"First you must be more precise about what brought you here, madam," Susan told her. "If you would not delay to state your business, I would be deeply grateful."

"We know that he has declared for you and that you have accepted!" Lady Knightly cried.

"He has not declared. I have not accepted," Susan said firmly, hoping against hope that Sir Rupert had not been explicit about their encounter in the rose garden.

"Are you calling my son a liar, Miss Eaton?" Lady Knightly exclaimed, taking further recourse to her vinaigrette.

"Perhaps he has great powers of imagination," Susan told her. "I repeat. He has not declared. I have not accepted. Indeed, I will go further.

Were he to declare, I would reject him in an instant. I hope I have made myself quite clear."

"She hopes to put us off until she has convinced him to elope as poor Maria did," Lady Woodstone hissed in her friend's ear.

Susan raised both hands in a gesture of impatience.

"What can I do to convince you?" she cried. "No doubt there are some who would find Sir Rupert . . . interesting. I assure you that I am not one of them. No doubt there are some who would find him eligible. I am not among them. I cannot think why he has told you otherwise, but you must take my word for it. I mean to elope with no one, least of all your son, Lady Knightly."

"Oh, you are clever, my girl!" Lady Woodstone said, rising. "You hope to delude us until Rupert is so firmly captured that there is no help for a marriage between you. He knows already that your father is away from home today, but as soon as he returns the poor boy means to come here and make an avowal. You know that then it will be too late for us to intervene."

"How should Sir Rupert know anything of my father's whereabouts?" Susan demanded.

"Our footman told him," Lady Woodstone declared. "He has, I think, some source of information in the village."

"Indeed he has," Susan said grimly. "And it would be better for us all if he had not. You are correct in thinking my father gone at present.

You do not know how relieved I am that he is not here. But on his return I will inform him of my firm intention not to accept Sir Rupert's offer."

"A likely thing!" Lady Knightly cried, following her friend to the parlor door. "Play your games, Miss Eaton! But you must know that I will never accept anyone like you as daughter-in-law! It is unthinkable! I will never . . ."

She broke off with an expression of alarm as Franklin appeared in the doorway. His face was as grim as his appearance was unexpected.

"I believe that apologies are in order," he said.

Jane gave a little cry and reached out to clasp Susan's hand. Both girls stared at the young man in amazement and the two older ladies appeared to be no less disconcerted.

"You will both apologize to my sister before you leave this house," Franklin said and it was clear from the way in which he held himself that he was in a fury. "And when Sir Rupert comes here—if, indeed, he does—he will apologize as well or face me with a pistol in his hand tomorrow at dawn."

"Why, he is mad!" Lady Knightly cried, clutching Lady Woodstone's arm.

"Stand out of our way, young man," Lady Woodstone declared, her voice wavering.

"Apologize, madam." Franklin repeated. "Apologize, or I will not be responsible."

Hesitantly, Lady Woodstone turned to face Susan. Her face was as gray as smoke.

"If my friend and I have misjudged you, Miss Eaton, we are sorry," she murmured.

"Yes, yes. We are sorry," Lady Knightly whispered. "Only tell him to let us go!"

"Step aside, Franklin, do!" Susan implored her brother.

For a moment Franklin considered. And then he moved to one side. The two ladies scuttled past him like twin spiders. The front door opened. Closed.

"Franklin!" Susan said in an awed voice.

"Franklin!" Jane cried adoringly.

A broad smile creased the young man's cheeks as both girls hurled themselves at him.

CHAPTER
Eighteen

"*I know that Franklin* means well, Papa," Susan told her father an hour later. "But, really, have you ever heard such foolishness? He must be prevented from challenging Sir Rupert to a duel at all costs!"

Squire Eaton appeared to give the matter judicious thought. They were sitting in his study, a narrow, booklined room, the windows of which gave rather too good a view, in Susan's present state of mind, of the south meadow. Indeed, she had deliberately seated herself with her back to the windows in order to prevent being reminded of her disastrous meeting there with Patience that morning. What folly that encounter had produced, and no one to blame but herself.

"It seems an odd thing to me that this Sir Rupert should have taken so much upon him with no encouragement from you, my dear," her father said slowly. "Unless, of course, the man is mad which, given what you have told me, I am quite prepared to believe."

Susan flushed. It had been one thing to keep her mother as much in the dark as possible and quite another to gloss over certain facts with her father who, above all, preferred to deal with facts.

"If, as you fear, Sir Rupert may be coming here for an interview with me directly, I should not be taken by surprise by anything he has to say," the squire said gently.

"Well, as for that," Susan said, raising her head and looking her parent straight in the eyes, "I may have been a bit to blame."

"You flirted with the gentleman, then?"

"Never!" Susan assured him.

"Then surely, my dear, you are to blame for nothing."

"Oh, but I was foolish," Susan assured him, determined to be completely frank. "You see, I met the Misses Reardon's maid Patience in the south meadow this morning. I was on a walk and she—well, she was just returning from meeting a—a friend from Muir Hall."

She hesitated and then decided that there was no special virtue to be attached to complete honesty as far as Patience was concerned. Not that she had any reason to protect the girl, but surely her relationship with Lord Woodstone's footman was a private matter.

"Patience told me," she continued, "that she thought she knew where Maria Woodstone and her lieutenant had eloped to. And since I knew that Lord Woodstone is most eager to determine his sister's address . . . well, it occurred to me to drop by the Hall and tell him, since I was so close."

"I see," her father said and, from the look in his eyes, Susan was afraid that he saw even more than she had intended him to.

"That was my mistake, you see," she went on swiftly, eager to provide distraction. "I went through the gap in the wall into the rose garden, expecting to find him there. Patience had told me that he was spending the morning making plans for improving the garden and . . ."

How easy it was when one was disconcerted to fumble with one's words, she thought, forcing herself to go on, hoping that she would say neither too much nor too little.

"I am certain that your mother would say that such an informal visit to Muir Hall was not quite proper," the squire said slowly, "but I think I understand why it was made."

Certain now that he understood too much, Susan flushed.

"I meant to give Lord Woodstone the message and go away at once," she protested. "But, as it happened, he was not in the garden."

"And Sir Rupert was?" her father said in a low, speculative voice.

"Yes, Papa."

"You made no attempt to linger, I should hope."

He was severe now and Susan knew that she must hide nothing from him.

"He would not let me leave," she whispered.

"What!" her father cried, starting from his chair. "Do you mean that the fellow laid his hands on you?"

"Not at first," Susan said quickly. "He simply pretended to believe that I had come to see him. I told him I had not. I begged him to step out of my way. He accused me of being coy. He said he meant to declare for me. I told him I had no regard for him. And then . . ."

"I must know everything!" the squire thundered, standing over her.

"He attempted to embrace me," Susan whispered. "And then—then I managed to dart past him and make my escape. It was after that that he must have told his mother and Lady Woodstone that we were affianced."

"The cad!" the squire shouted. "Does your brother know all this? For if he does, I can understand why he intends to challenge. That fellow deserves to be horsewhipped. If he dares to come within an arm's length of me, I shall do so!"

Susan stared at him in dismay. How could it have come to this? Her brother spoke of a duel and her father of horsewhipping. She closed her eyes and begged the Fates to keep Sir Rupert a far distance from this house.

Leaving her father fuming to himself with an occasional pause to pound the desk, Susan hurried up the stairs to Franklin's room. Seeing the door ajar, she pushed it open to her brother sitting on the edge of his bed, intent on polishing a pistol of ancient vintage. He looked up at the sound of her gasp and assumed the stubborn expression which she knew all too well.

"Where did you get that, Frank?" Susan demanded.

For a moment she thought that he was not about to deign to answer her for he resumed his polishing with a will, avoiding her eyes.

"Found it in a trunk in the attic," she heard him mutter. "Belonged to Grandfather."

"Surely you do not intend to use it!" Susan exclaimed in dismay. "Why, for all you know it may have been so long out of use that it will backfire on you!"

She caught herself short then, realizing that his folly had led her to one of her own.

"What I mean to say is that you must not use that pistol or any other," she went on hastily. "I have just now spoken to Father and he will attend to Sir Rupert in his own way."

"And I will attend to him in mine," Franklin assured her, rubbing the long barrel of the gun with more energy than before.

"It was all a foolish error," Susan pleaded. "Believe me, Franklin, there is no need for dramatics. It is a tempest in a teapot. Sir Rupert is a fool, granted, but that is no reason for you to be one as well."

Placing the pistol carefully on the table beside his bed, Franklin rose ponderously, took her arm, and ushered her unceremoniously out the door. Raging silently against the determination of both her father and brother, and with a rising sense of anxiety, Susan ran down the stairs and out into the garden where she peered anxiously down the road in the direction of Muir Hall. When she had run from the rose garden she had had no intention of ever speaking a word to Sir Rupert again, but now she found herself hoping against hope that, if he meant to come, it would be *now* so that she could warn him. True he had behaved outrageously toward her but she could not stand by and see him horsewhipped or, even worse, shot.

Her heart began to race as she heard the sound of horse's hooves thudding against the dry dirt of the road, but it was only a wagon driven by Luck Hakket. After that there was a dreadful silence. And then she saw a horseman approach. One anxious minute passed and then another before she saw that it was Sir Rupert seated on one of Lord Woodstone's grays.

She ran to meet him, praying that no one would see her.

"Damme, this is a fine surprise," Sir Rupert declared as she approached him. He reined his horse and dismounted, a grin creasing his broad face. "Been waiting for me, have you, Miss

Eaton. Told Mother she and that friend of hers had it all wrong. 'The gel's playing coy,' I said. 'Don't talk to me about what she says. It's what she does that proves the point. Once she sees that I mean to speak to her father she'll be keen enough.' That's what I told them, but would they listen? Hysterics all over the place. Foolish notions. Talk of apology and such. Muckworms, both of them, which is what I said straight out."

Susan carefully placed herself at arm's reach from him and tried not to be disconcerted either by his leer or by his words.

"I have come to warn you, Sir Rupert," she said evenly. "You must forget all these foolish fancies of yours at once and listen to me."

"There's a bit of coyness left yet, eh?" the young man declared delightedly. " 'Pon my word, I always said a feast was the better for the waiting on it. Know how to play a fellow like a trout, indeed you do, Miss Eaton. Have to put an end to this nonsense when were properly engaged, you know. That's when I'll want a bit of affection, if you take my meaning."

At that happy thought he grinned in such an awful manner that it was all that Susan could do to keep her countenance.

"There *is* to be no engagement," she told him. "I have told my father what to say to you. I refuse any offer that you make. But that is not what I came out to tell you. If you take even one more step toward my house, you will be in grave danger!"

"Danger of being accepted you mean!" Sir Rupert chortled. "Like a sense of humor! Yes, that's fine! Fine!"

"Even as it is Franklin will see you if he happens to look out his chamber window," Susan went on, speaking very slowly and carefully as she might have done had Sir Rupert been deaf which, in a sense, he was.

"Franklin?" Sir Rupert demanded. "What has he to do with anything? I thought the fellow kept himself locked in his room of late."

He scratched his head. "Now that you mention it," he went on, "there was some talk of his making an appearance this afternoon when the two ladies made their visit. Missed most of what they said in the general excitement, don't you know. Took it they had seen him, however. Wanted them to apologize for something or other, I forget what."

"You forget what!" Susan exclaimed impatiently. "Why, they insulted me. But that is not the point. The fact is . . ."

"Insulted you, did they?" Sir Rupert interrupted. "Well, then, your brother was quite right. Can't have that you know. Insult my intended! 'Pon my word, I never heard of such a thing. They'll have the rough edge of my tongue when I return to Muir Hall, I'll tell you that."

"Forget the insults!" Susan cried. "What matters is that when I told my father what had happened in the garden . . ."

"Told him that, did you?" Sir Rupert said,

198

leering again. "Called you a saucy little baggage, I imagine. Doesn't do to be too open when it comes to romance, you know. Private matters! Private matters! In future we must have our little secrets, don't you know."

"Why can't you listen!" Susan exclaimed, stamping her foot. "My father knows that you accosted me against my will. He's in a fury. Do you understand me? Can you comprehend that, at least? He is in a fury and promises to greet you with a horsewhip! And do not think I care except that it would cause such a scandal that we would never be able to live it down."

"Horsewhip?" Sir Rupert said, clearly puzzled. "What's a horsewhip to do with this?"

"He means to beat you with it," Susan said in despair. "Only try to understand."

"Beat me with a horsewhip," Sir Rupert repeated. "Why, I'm a gentleman. That simply isn't done."

"It will be if Father sees you," Susan promised him. "And then there is my brother. He intends to challenge you to a duel."

"A duel?" Sir Rupert said vacantly. "Oh, I see! This is another of your little jokes, Miss Eaton. What a card you are, to be sure."

"I am *not* attempting to be funny," Susan told him in a perfect fit of impatience. "Get back on your horse at once, I beg you. Return to Muir Hall. Better yet, return to London."

But she saw that his attention had been distracted.

"There's your brother now," he said. "We'll have a good laugh about this together."

With a cry, Susan turned and saw Franklin striding toward them. In one hand he held a single glove, one of the white gloves which he wore for dancing. It must, she thought, have been the first one to come to hand when he had seen her and Sir Rupert from the window and she knew all too well what he intended to do with it.

"Franklin! No!" she cried.

But Franklin was upon them, pushing his way between her and Sir Rupert.

"Such Banbury stories as your sister has been telling me," Sir Rupert began.

But he had no time to finish for just at that instant Franklin struck him a blow across the face with the white glove.

"Damme, what do you think you're doing?" Sir Rupert exclaimed.

"I am insulting you as your mother insulted my sister, sir," Franklin said fiercely. "We will meet in the south meadow inside the hour. Pistols, sir! Make sure you come prepared, or I will seek you out like the dirty dog you are!"

And with that he took Susan by the arm and propelled her none too gently back down the road in the direction of the house.

CHAPTER
Nineteen

"*But duels are meant* to be had at sunrise, I always thought," Jane Dawson said with an irrelevance born of shock.

"Surely that is beside the point," Susan said with some asperity. "Father has argued with Franklin and so has Mama, for we could not keep it from her. But nothing can sway him. Why, when Papa threatened to lock him in his room, he said he would take to the window, if necessary. And all the time they talked, he sat there on his bed polishing and oiling that ghastly old pistol."

Jane Dawson walked to the window of the sitting room, wringing her hands. "Papa is having a word with him now," she said, "although what good it will do I do not know."

"If your father is taking the line of Christian

duty toward his fellow man, I doubt if he will elicit much response," Susan said grimly. "Franklin is in no mood for sermons."

"Cannot someone send for the constable?" Jane demanded. "Surely he would put a stop to this."

"Sam Toliver is away on a trip to Exeter to visit his old mother," Susan told her. "I thought of sending for the garrison, but Papa said they would not feel they had a right to interfere in a private matter such as this."

"Well, there is this," Jane said with a faint ray of hope in her eyes. "You said that Sir Rupert was too astounded to say anything when Franklin struck him with his glove. Perhaps he does not mean to keep the appointment. I thought that titled gentlemen only dueled with their equals."

"I had thought of that," Susan assured her. "No message has come from Muir Hall, at any rate. He might refuse to accept the challenge for the reason you mentioned, or from lack of courage. We cannot hope that Sir Rupert will refuse because of common sense, however. That is too much to expect, I fear."

"Ah, but the same cannot be said of Lord Woodstone," Jane declared with an air of triumph. "Why did I not think of him before. Surely he will not allow Sir Rupert to take part in this charade."

Although the same hope had been ranging Susan's mind for the past hour, she made no reply. She hoped that what Jane suggested might be true. But, oh, what a bitter humiliation it was for her that Lord Woodstone would see her brother for the impetuous fool he was. And, as for her, what could he think but that she had led Sir Rupert on and been, of a consequence, the source of all this trouble?

"Patience is coming!" Jane exclaimed, leaning closer to the window. "See, she is running down the road."

In a moment the Misses Reardon's maid had joined the two girls in the sitting room, having entered by the front door in her haste and pushing Sally aside. As she fought to catch her breath, Susan fought the impulse to rebuke her for having given the advice she had that morning. At the same time she remembered that in the crush of the day's events she had not managed to inform Lord Woodstone of his sister's whereabouts. How unimportant all that seemed just now.

Patience's red curls had tumbled from beneath her cap and she clutched her waist with one hand, declaring that she had given herself a stitch.

"But the Misses Reardon thought that you should know what was going on at Muir Hall, miss," she said to Susan. "Tom came to tell me that they are at sixes and sevens, everyone talking at once and swooning and such."

"Then Sir Rupert means to accept the challenge," Susan said in a low voice.

"He is target shooting in the garden at this moment, miss," Patience replied. "Tom says he is an uncertain shot at best and that he has already knocked the head off the statue of Apollo and accidentally killed a peacock."

With a cry, Jane threw herself onto a chair and began to wail softly.

"Tom says that we can only hope that he intends to take a fair aim at your brother and not try to shoot over his head," Patience went on excitedly, "since what he aims at he always misses."

"And Franklin has never, to my knowledge, fired a gun in his life," Susan said gloomily. "No doubt they will both dispatch one another with no delay. Papa must think of something to keep Franklin from the field, since it seems that Lord Woodstone has decided to do nothing. Perhaps he intends to be Sir Rupert's second."

"Lord Woodstone is not at home, Miss," Patience said, clearly delighted to offer still more information. "Tom says he went off late this morning in a rage about something. He said nothing of where he was going or when he could be expected to return."

Susan turned aside, knowing that her face was draining of its color. If Lord Woodstone was in a rage, she knew the reason why. Once again she remembered the expression in his eyes when he had found her in Sir Rupert's arms. He had thought her a friend and now believed her to be something yet again. He had thought her sensible and found her wanton. Her shame was like a burning coal inside her throat and, for a moment, she could not speak.

She felt Jane's arm about her shoulder.

"Perhaps he will return in time to put a stop to this," her friend said gently, having collected herself, clearly determined to have hope until the last.

"The whole village is agog, miss," Patience declared. "Why, the Misses Reardon are decking themselves out in their best this very moment and Mrs. Jackson and her daughters, too."

"I suppose you have been busy spreading the word," Susan said bitterly.

"It is what everyone has come to expect of me, miss," Patience said simply. "Besides, this sort of news spreads itself."

"You do not mean the entire village intends to come and watch?" Jane declared, appalled. "Will they make some sort of ghastly fete of this!"

"Everyone is most anxious for Mr. Franklin," Patience assured her. "Knowing human nature as I do, I expect that some will come out of simple curiosity, but his friends are anxious for him. Surely you would not expect them to stay away."

Difficult though it was for Susan to be particularly genial to anyone under the circumstances and, in particular, to someone who had, albeit unwittingly, caused her so much trouble, she thanked Patience for coming with news of the goings-on at Muir Hall and urged her to hurry back to her elderly mistresses with the word that the duel would be prevented at all cost.

"Although who is to do that, I do not know," she said hopelessly as the door closed behind the redhaired maid. "We can only hope that Franklin has listened to your father, Jane, since it is, apparently, to be our last hope."

But when, a moment later, she saw Parson Dawson's face as he descended the stairs with her mother and father in attendance, Susan knew that he, too, had failed.

"Never have I seen anyone so adamant," the parson said, wiping his forehead with his handkerchief.

"Oh, 'tis folly! Folly!" Mrs. Eaton cried, clearly quite beside herself. "He will be killed, I know it! You must do something, my dear! Anything!"

"There is nothing more than I can do," her husband said heavily. "This is what comes of my having let him have his way in so many other matters. He has never learned to listen to reason and this is the consequence."

They all grew silent as steps were heard on the stairs. Every head turned to observe Franklin as he descended with an awful air of dignity. No knight in armor could have made a more imposing sight than he did with his shoulders squared under the dark brown superfine of a jacket which sported a velvet collar. In apparent uncertainty as to the correct costume for an afternoon contest with pistols, Franklin had decked himself in a white pique waistcoat and tied his cravat as fancifully as any dandy. His topboots glistened from a recent polishing, as did the pistol which he had seen fit not to carry in a case. A further incongruous note was established by the beaver hat which he wore jauntily on one side of his head. Had it not been for the pistol, Susan thought, it might have seemed that he was off for an afternoon of whist at the Misses Reardon's.

"Oh, Franklin!" she heard Jane whisper.

As her brother stopped on the next to the last step and surveyed them, Susan knew that she must make one last attempt to stop him.

"You know, of course," she said firmly, "that if you proceed you will break Mama's heart."

Franklin seemed unmoved.

"It is a matter of honor," he said.

"Add to that the fact that you will make me the center of a public scandal," Susan went on.

"There is scandal enough already," Franklin said, his eyes focused on the middle distance like someone in a trance.

"You are playing the fool," Susan told him in complete exasperation. "And you have had the misfortune to encounter another who is as great an idiot as you."

"How can you be so harsh, my dear?" Mrs. Eaton said faintly. "Your brother may be wrong, but he believes himself to be right. Surely you can see that. La, this is a nightmare, indeed it is. I feel quite giddy."

"Help your mistress to the sofa and fetch her vinaigrette," Mr. Eaton said to Sally with a strange, harsh quality in his voice. "Come,

Franklin. Listen to reason. Everything your sister says is true."

But Franklin had turned his attention on Jane Dawson who stood staring at him with tears coursing down her cheeks.

"If I could have a token," he said in a low voice, approaching her.

For a moment it was clear that Jane could not think what he meant. And then she slowly pulled off the ribbon which bound her curls and handed it to him. It came to Susan in that instant that her brother was a romantic of the first water. He stared at stars, formed hopeless attachments, and now he clearly saw himself as a knight about to enter the contest with his lady's favor tucked inside his pocket. Asking Jane for a token was a declaration of affection for her and Susan could only hope that her dear friend saw it for the important gesture that it was. Indeed, Jane seemed to understand for, although her eyes still glistened with tears, there was a new expression in them, one of delight and hope intermingled. For a moment Franklin's hand lingered on hers as he took the ribbon and then he turned smartly on his heel and marched out the door.

CHAPTER
Twenty

$\mathcal{F}$*ollowing her brother* outside, with Jane Dawson close behind her, Susan was appalled to see that the entire village had apparently been waiting for this moment. Because of what Patience had told her, she was not unduly surprised to see the Misses Reardon both neatly arrayed in their best gray silk afternoon gowns coming down the road, their poke bonnets touching as they chattered excitedly to one another. And, given the circumstances, it was only to be expected that Mrs. Jackson, together with Ruth and Priscilla should come hurrying after.

But the procession did not end there. Indeed, it had scarcely begun. Captain Blazemore, erect in his frockcoat, marched along with the military precision of an old soldier in the company of

Mr. and Mrs. Lawson and behind them, streaming in a ragged line, came the blacksmith and the greengrocer, both accompanied by their wives and so many others that the village must have been left a ghost town. True, there was no fete-like atmosphere, for everyone spoke in whispers, and, as they turned onto the lane which led to the south meadow, many were the condolences which were extended to the little group standing on the squire's front steps.

"So sad!" the Misses Reardon offered in unison.

"Too terrible for words!" Mrs. Jackson said as her daughters nodded their heads emphatically.

"Young gentlemen will get their blood up," Captain Blazemore observed. "It's the way of the world."

"We cannot stay here, Papa!" Susan exclaimed. "If anything should happen to Frank, we must be on hand to help him."

"The young rascal does not even have a second," her father grumbled, trying as best he could to hide his anguish. "Very well, then. I'll be off. You'll come with me, Parson?"

"I'll offer prayers," the cleric declared emphatically. "The hand of heaven . . ."

"We must go, too, Susan," Jane whispered as her father hurried after Squire Eaton. "I do not know how I can bear to watch and yet it would be even worse to stay here and not know what was happening."

Susan took a deep breath. There was nothing

to keep her. Sally was attending to her mother far more competently than she could do. And, as Jane said, it would be unendurable to wait. And yet she dreaded the intensification of the frustration she already felt. She did not know if she could remain silent when her brother faced Sir Rupert. She knew she might not be able to control herself and, in so doing, make further scandel by her own behavior. And yet she must go. And bear the guilt for whatever might happen.

With a nod of agreement, she started toward the meadow lane, not bothering to fetch a bonnet. And, as she did so, a phaeton came racing down the road from the direction of the village and a familiar voice hailed her. Turning, she saw Lieutenant Moore at the reins of the conveyance with Maria beside him.

"Whatever is going on?" the girl cried. "The village is deserted!"

Instantly, Susan knew what she must do. Hurrying to the side of the now stationary phaeton with Jane breathless at her heels, she made a rapid explanation.

"But, whyever should your brother fight Rupert?" Maria declared in a state of high excitement. "Rupert never meant anything to me."

She was, Susan thought, more beautiful than ever with the bridal glow still shining in her eyes. But nothing had changed her obtuseness, although it was clear from the adoring way in which her young husband looked at her that this fault did not bother him.

"The quarrel is over something else," Susan said shortly. "But one of them will kill the other unless someone can stop them. Your brother is the man to do it, Maria. But he cannot be found. He knows nothing of this. You know his ways. He was troubled about something and went for a ride this morning. If you have any notion where he might be . . ."

"I should not like to see Franklin hurt," Maria declared. "Nor Rupert either, although he is quite tiresome at times."

"Do you think you might be able to find your brother?" Susan insisted. And then, casting all modesty to the winds: "Tell him that I beg him to come at once. In the meantime I will see what delay can be made."

"You can count on me to try," Maria said cheerfully. "I know that when James could bear no more of Mama and me, he often went to a certain place not far from here. And Carl drives like the wind, don't you, darling?"

Lieutenant Moore's response was to clap the reins against the horse's flanks with such enthusiasm that the phaeton literally shot off down the road with Maria crying out reassurances while clasping her pink bonnet to her head with both hands.

"How like her to turn up at a time like this," Jane declared.

"We cannot depend on her to be able to help," Susan said grimly. "Keep that in mind. Do not raise your hopes. And now we must hurry and try to see to it that there is some delay."

The scene which met their eyes as they mounted to the crest of the south meadow was not reassuring. Franklin stood beneath the oak tree, apparently intent on loading his pistol while his father and Parson Dawson spoke to him earnestly, and the inhabitants of the village formed a ragged half circle about him. Further on, Sir Rupert stood examining his own weapon which he had apparently just removed from a case which Tom held out to him. Nor were they alone for the entire servant staff of Muir Hall had turned out for the event and, in the midst of them, leaning against one another for support, stood Lady Woodstone, Lady Knightly and Drusella, each with vinaigrettes in their hands.

"What do you intend to do?" Jane demanded as Susan made her way around the villagers and started toward Sir Rupert. "Surely you do not intend to speak to *him*! Not now! Not here! It will seem a betrayal of your brother!"

"I will betray myself if necessary," Susan assured her grimly. "If worse comes to worse, I will tell him that I accept his offer. There can be no duel then, since he can scarcely turn his pistol against the brother of the lady to whom he is affianced."

"You would do that!" Jane exclaimed as they hurried across the grass. It was clear that they had become the focus of attention, for the villagers had grown quite silent and cries of

213

denunciation rose from the three ladies on the other side.

"Damme, what are you doing here?" Sir Rupert demanded as Susan came up to him. "Not quite the thing, you know! Not quite the thing!"

"I—I only wanted to remind you that these affairs must be managed properly," Susan said in a low voice. "As for my brother, he is not a man of the world such as you. And everything has been arranged in such haste that I imagine certain proprieties have been forgotten even by you, sir."

"Proprieties!" Sir Rupert exclaimed. "Why, I have answered his challenge, which is more than he deserves. And I have my second here."

"But my brother does not," Susan told him. "Simply because my father and Parson Dawson are standing by him does not mean that either has agreed to second him. You know the niceties of dueling far better than I, sir, and you are aware, I think, that the seconds must make the arrangements as to distance and—and that sort of thing. Furthermore, a physician must be in attendance and, to my certain knowledge, Dr. Wayland is at home taking his usual afternoon nap."

"Well, as for that, it was your brother's duty to provide for both a second and a doctor," Sir Rupert said in an outraged voice. "He made the challenge, Miss Eaton! And now you tell me he has not made the proper arrangements. Why, this is quite impossible!"

"I think that you should send Tom to tell him

so," Susan replied. "It will take some little time, perhaps, for Frank to find someone to serve as his second but no doubt it will be possible. As for the doctor, I think you will agree he must be sent for. If the word should ever reach your friends in London that you had agreed to fight a duel in such a ragtaggle manner as now exists, I think you would find yourself a laughingstock."

"Damme, of course I would!" Sir Rupert replied. "Can't thank you enough, Miss Eaton, for having taken the trouble. Off with you, Tom! Tell the fellow I will not agree to take a single shot at him until affairs are put on a better standing than this!"

A period of confusion ensued, during which Tom could be seen in earnest consultation with Franklin, following which young Jack Hiddle, the blacksmith's boy, was sent running to the village to fetch the doctor, and Captain Blazemore, nothing loath, was prevailed upon to be Franklin's second.

Meanwhile Susan and Jane joined the cluster of Franklin's supporters who were chattering excitedly about the turn of events.

"La, I wonder you could bring yourself to speak to Sir Rupert, my dear!" Miss Martha Reardon declared, fanning herself with her handkerchief.

"I thought you had decided to accept his offer," said Miss Willamena. "I said to Martha, I said, 'There, the gel's gone and changed her mind at the last minute.'"

"And a good thing it would have been if you had, to my way of thinking," declared Mrs. Jackson, while on either side her daughters nodded their heads like wilted daffodils in the wind. "Only fancy, turning down a gentleman with a handle to his name!"

Franklin, who had been listening to Captain Blazemore hold forth with a certain impatience, chose this moment to turn in Jane's direction; whereupon, having her full attention, he took her ribbon from his pocket and held it meaningfully to his heart.

"He has come to his senses in one regard, at least," Susan said dryly as her friend's hand tightened on hers. "Now we must hope that Dr. Wayland will not be at home. Either that, or so sound asleep that the boy will not be able to rouse him by knocking at the door. Any delay will be for the good."

"But do you think that even if Maria can find her brother, he will take steps?" Jane demanded urgently. "Oh, Susan. I could not bear it if anything should happen to Franklin now!"

"If Lord Woodstone knows what is happening, he will come," Susan said. "I am certain of that, if nothing else."

"But even if he does come, what can he possibly do?" Jane whispered, aware that the Misses Reardon were bending their ears in their direction.

"He is ingenious enough to think of something," Susan assured her. "But we should not raise our hopes too high. See, here is the doctor now."

Dr. Wayland was a very old man indeed and it was clear from the expression on his wrinkled face that he was not altogether pleased at having been routed from his bed. Indeed, he showed every sign of having dressed himself hastily, for the periwig which he affected was set on one side of his head and his ancient frockcoat was unbuttoned. Still, he had clearly come prepared, for he carried his little black bag full of antiquated instruments and, as he passed her, Susan heard him mutter something about stuff and nonsense.

Her heart sinking now that the time had well and truly come, Susan detached herself from Jane and hurried to her father's side. The squire was clearly in the throes of the most intense frustration, for he paced back and forth, beating his hands together and mumbling to himself.

"Can you not think of something that will change Frank's mind, Papa?" Susan demanded.

"If he were ten years younger I would thrash him black and blue," the squire told her. "I blame myself for this. I spoiled him as a lad and look what has come of it. How I shall ever face his mother after this I do not know."

"She spoiled him, too, Papa," Susan said, taking one of his hands between her own and fondling it. "And so did I. But it is his own foolhardiness which is most to blame."

A great silence fell upon the crowd now as Captain Blazemore walked with military dignity to meet Tom by the beech tree, and the ritual began. After a few minutes' conversation, each returned to the gentleman whose second he was, and still another discussion took place. Already wearied by the proceedings, Dr. Wayland leaned against the blacksmith's boy and seemed about to resume his nap, while all about him the air turned electric with the general tension.

Susan had never seen a duel before but she had read a great sufficiency about them in novels and she knew that the seconds had determined, among other things, how far the two armed gentleman should stand from one another. Still, it came as a shock to her when the proceedings actually began. Slowly and with considerable dignity, Franklin and Sir Rupert strode toward one another, pistols pointed toward the ground. A little murmur rose from the village side as they met beneath the beech tree. For a moment they stood staring at one another and then, at a word from Captain Blazemore who stood at one side, they turned their backs on one another and began to pace off the distance that would separate them when it was time to fire.

Time seemed to be suspended, Susan thought, as she held her breath. Franklin and Sir Rupert turned at the same moment. Each raised his pistol. From the other side of the field a woman screamed and Susan imagined that Lady Knightly had chosen this moment to collapse. The pistols came to rest, each at the end of an outstretched arm. Both seemed to quiver as

218

though the hand of neither gentleman was altogether steady. In a moment Susan knew that she would hear two shots.

But only one sounded.

The bullet struck the beech tree, shattering bark from its side.

Someone else had fired!

Heads turned and a confused roar of voices rose from either side of the field as a horse and rider appeared from the direction of Muir Hall. It was Lord Woodstone who came galloping toward them, a smoking pistol in his hand. Susan took a deep breath and pressed her cold hands to her cheeks.

"Have done with this, you fools!" she heard him shout as he reined his horse at midpoint between the two duellists. Sir Rupert and Franklin stared at him blankly and then, as one man, dropped their own weapons to the ground.

"And now," Lord Woodstone said in a voice which seemed to carry the width and breadth of the meadow, "I want an explanation!"

With heads bowed, Sir Rupert and Franklin approached him. They spoke, at first reluctantly and then with urgency and Lord Woodstone listened. When he had apparently heard enough, he turned his horse and searched the faces of the still silent spectators until he saw Susan.

"Miss Eaton will decide," he announced, his dark eyes hooded. "Since this matter concerns her honor, she will decide if the duel is to be continued."

Susan stepped forward, leaving her father, leaving everyone and, as she did so, Lord Woodstone dismounted and came toward her. She paused when there were still some ten paces between them.

"No," she said clearly. "There will be no duel."

Pandemonium followed. The villagers encircled Franklin, clapping him on the back and shaking his hand, while the occupants of Muir Hall, joined by a flushed and windblown Maria together with her husband, congratulated Sir Rupert in like manner. Only Patience and Tom took advantage of the situation to slip away, hand in hand.

All this Susan noted with but a part of her attention. She and Lord Woodstone stood away from the others and his eyes held her with their urgency.

"I must beg your pardon for misinterpreting what I saw in the rose garden," he said in a low voice. "Sir Rupert has confessed to everything. He admits to having been a fool and worse."

"None of us are blameless," Susan told him. "I have been impetuous."

"And I have mistrusted where there should have been no doubt," he told her, moving closer until only a narrow strip of meadow grass swayed in the breeze between them.

"I knew you faulted me for Maria's elopement," Susan said.

"If I faulted you for anything, I was wrong,"

he murmured. "Tell me. Can you ever forgive me for having doubted you in anything?"

Her smile told him everything. Hand in hand they wandered off across the meadow, their eyes on one another's faces until they were so far away that even the shrill voices of the Misses Reardon and Lady Woodstone could not reach them.

"We have, I think, a deal to say to one another," Lord Woodstone said in a low voice.

"We have everything to say," Susan told him. "I wonder if there will ever be time to say it all."

"We will make a beginning now," he murmured, gently drawing her into his arms, quite oblivious to the fact that back under the beech tree, Lady Knightly and Lady Woodstone had jointly succumbed to the vapors, while Drusella collapsed in a fit of laughter and the Misses Reardon, together with Mrs. Jackson and her daughter, set up a great buzz of gossip. As for Squire Eaton, he surveyed the distant couple with an air of satisfaction and Franklin, with Jane Dawson hanging on his arm, extended his hand to Sir Rupert who shook it with considerable enthusiasm.

And somewhere in the shade of a certain willow tree, Patience stirred in Tom's embrace.

"What a fuss the gentry make of love," she said cheerfully. "Faith, there's nothing in the world more simple."

MASTER NOVELISTS

CHESAPEAKE CB 24163 $3.95
by James A. Michener

An enthralling historical saga. It gives the account of different generations and races of American families who struggled, invented, endured and triumphed on Maryland's Chesapeake Bay. It is the first work of fiction in ten years to be first on *The New York Times Best Seller List*.

THE BEST PLACE TO BE PB 04024 $2.50
by Helen Van Slyke

Sheila Callaghan's husband suddenly died, her children are grown, independent and troubled, the men she meets expect an easy kind of woman. Is there a place of comfort? a place for strength against an aching void? A novel for every woman who has ever loved.

ONE FEARFUL YELLOW EYE GB 14146 $1.95
by John D. MacDonald

Dr. Fortner Geis relinquishes $600,000 to someone that no one knows. Who knows his reasons? There is a history of threats which Travis McGee exposes. But why does the full explanation live behind the eerie yellow eye of a mutilated corpse?

8002

GREAT ROMANTIC NOVELS

SISTERS AND STRANGERS   PB 04445 $2.50
by Helen Van Slyke
     Three women—three sisters each grown into an independent lifestyle—now are three strangers who reunite to find that their intimate feelings and perilous fates are entwined.

THE SUMMER OF THE SPANISH WOMAN
                                   CB 23809 $2.50
by Catherine Gaskin
     A young, fervent Irish beauty is alone. The only man she ever loved is lost as is the ancient family estate. She flees to Spain. There she unexpectedly discovers the simmering secrets of her wretched past . . . meets the Spanish Woman . . . and plots revenge.

THE CURSE OF THE KINGS   CB 23284 $1.95
by Victoria Holt
     This is Victoria Holt's most exotic novel! It is a story of romance when Judith marries Tybalt, the young archeologist, and they set out to explore the Pharaohs' tombs on their honeymoon. But the tombs are cursed . . . two archeologists have already died mysteriously.

8000